Home

A Novel

Adrienne Thompson

Pink Cashmere Publishing, LLC

Arkansas, USA

Cover Art by A. A. Thompson (thompson9699@gmail.com)

Printed in the United States of America

First Printing 2015

Copyright © 2015 Adrienne Thompson

ISBN: 0988871394

ISBN-13: 978-0-9888713-9-7

Thank You, Lord, for everything and all things. For loving me, for keeping me, for strengthening me, for favoring me.

Big thank you to my beta readers, Tonja Tate and Barbara Joe Williams. I deeply appreciate you!!

Thank you to all of my Facebook, Twitter, and Google+ friends for helping me spread the word about my books. There are too many of you to name, but you know who you are, and I hope you know how much I appreciate your support!!

This book is dedicated to the men in my life.

"Be kind to one another, tenderhearted, forgiving one another, as God in Christ forgave you."

Ephesians 4:32

Soundtrack:

"Again" *John Legend*

"The Beginning…" *John Legend*

"Coming Home" *John Legend*

"Good Morning" *John Legend*

"Green Light" *John Legend*

"Comin' From Where I'm From" *Anthony Hamilton*

"Hard Times" *John Legend & The Roots*

"Used To Love U" *John Legend*

"Dreams" *John Legend*

"Life Has a Way" *Anthony Hamilton*

"Better Days" *Anthony Hamilton*

"Another Again" *John Legend*

"Blame Me" *Jaheim*

"Baby Girl" *Anthony Hamilton*

"The Truth" *Anthony Hamilton*

"Sista Big Bones" *Anthony Hamilton*

"Since I Seen't You" *Anthony Hamilton*

"Just Don't Have A Clue" *Jaheim*

"Caught Up" *John Legend*

Listen to the Home Book Soundtrack Playlist on YouTube

Prologue

Mrs. Roundtree was my sixth grade teacher. Now, one thing you need to know about a twelve-year-old boy: anything can translate into sex. With Mrs. Roundtree, it was her smile. She had the sexiest smile. I don't think Mrs. Roundtree meant to be sexy. She just was. She had a talent for making everyone feel special with her smile. But to me, her smile said, "I want you, Ivan." I spent my days fantasizing about what it would be like to touch Mrs. Roundtree's legs. She always wore skirts and dresses and those soft, full legs mesmerized me. I wanted to taste those full lips of hers, too.

Once, I won a school-wide spelling bee, and Mrs. Roundtree hugged me. I dreamt about her soft body from that day forward. She hugged me again when I lost at district. See, she did care. When the school year was over, she kissed me on the cheek for being such a good student.

She was smart, too. She interjected a little black history into every lesson, whether it was math, English, or science. She taught me that black people could be whatever they wanted to be.

I never forgot Mrs. Roundtree or her mind or her body. She became the perfect model of a woman for me. A brown goddess with a good mind, a nice smile, nice legs, wide hips, and full breasts. She made me fall in love with women, brown women to be exact. So I think Mrs. Roundtree is to blame for me being the way I am. Yeah, it all started with her.

1

"Again"

I sat behind my huge desk and tried to keep my concentration while I rattled off a letter to Alma, my new secretary. Alma Lopez was half-Puerto Rican and half-Haitian. She was also young and attractive, and she knew it. Every other minute, she flipped her wavy, black hair over her shoulder or re-crossed her long, shapely legs, letting her short skirt ride up higher and higher. I shifted in my seat and told myself to stop looking at her. I knew women like Alma. They used scx to get what they wanted, and they usually succeeded. In the past, they'd *always* succeeded with me.

For years, I was an open book when it came to women. If you were young and attractive, you could easily get me. I loved women, no, let me correct that. I *love* women. The way they smell, the way they walk, their lips, *everything*. I've been incapable of resisting a beautiful woman for years. But, I'm proud to say that I hadn't given in to my weakness in weeks. I know that doesn't sound like much of an accomplishment, but for me it really was. I woke up one morning beside a lovely lady and decided I was tired of the flavor-of-the-night lifestyle I'd been living. Maybe it was time for me to settle down. Or maybe I was just tired.

I finished dictating the letter to Alma and smiled at her. "Okay, thanks, Alma. Be sure to have that letter ready by the morning."

She smiled seductively, or maybe that's just how it seemed to me. "Yes, sir. Um, Mr. Spencer? Can I ask you a question?"

I nodded. "Sure."

"Is it true that you were a rapper back in the day?"

Oh, that, I thought. Fame was like crack to women like Alma, even if it was faded fame. They'd do anything to get close to it. "Um, yes. But that was years ago," I said.

She lit up like a Pentecostal church. "Wow! When I got this job, my cousin told me you used to be Masta T.I.P. but I thought she was crazy. Then I looked on the internet, and I saw the pictures. I saw that it was you. This is great! I've never met a real live star before. Well, there was that time I saw Usher at a club, but I didn't get close to him."

I shrugged. "Well, I'd hardly call myself a star. I haven't performed in years. Real Estate is my thing now."

"Yeah, uh-huh. Do you still have any pictures, or anything from back in the day?" Alma wasn't paying a bit of attention to what I was saying.

"Alma, I don't think that'd be a good idea. Like I said, that was years ago. If you don't mind, I have some phone calls to make."

Her face fell. "Oh, okay." She left my office, closing the door behind her. I watched through the frosted glass of the door as she settled behind her own desk and dialed a number on her cell phone. My letter was forgotten as she engaged in a lively phone conversation.

I sighed. More than twenty years had passed, and Masta T.I.P. was still coming back to haunt me. But I suppose I couldn't expect to ever be able to totally shake that part of my life. I was a pretty successful rapper in the nineties. I made a lot of money and bedded a lot of women. Most men would've been glad to relive those glory days, but honestly, I was kind of ashamed of that period of my life. I owned a successful real estate agency despite the state of the economy. I was a respectable business man, and I wanted to be known for that, not a long-lost rap career. Hell, I didn't even listen to rap anymore. Give me a good John Legend CD any day.

I grabbed my cell phone and clipped it to my belt, shoved a few papers into my briefcase, and headed out of my office. As I stepped into the reception area, I stopped dead in my tracks. Alma was bent over, picking something up from the floor, and I had a full view of her butt. I loosened my tie and cleared my throat. "I'm heading out, Alma," I said.

She stood up straight and turned to look at me with a smile on her face. "Oh, okay. I'll lock up."

I nodded and headed toward the door. I started to open it and then stopped and turned around. "Um, Alma… if you'd like, you can come over to my house and have dinner with me tonight. I have a couple of photo albums full of pictures from back in the day. You can look to your heart's content."

She lit up again. "Really?!"

"Sure. What's your address? I'll pick you up around seven."

I never said I was perfect. I was still a work in progress, and Alma Lopez was too fine to miss out on.

2

"The Beginning…"

I sat there and tried not to let my eyes glaze over as another young, attractive, African American female rattled off her qualifications to me in an effort to convince me to hire her as my administrative assistant since, unfortunately, I'd had to fire Alma. One night was all I was trying to give her. But after that night, she started strutting around the office like she owned the place, typed on the keypad of her cell phone more than she ever did the computer. I just couldn't afford to keep her, or her attitude, around after I told her we were through.

So there I sat, just three months after hiring her, seeking her replacement, listening to Jazzmine, who was thicker than a six-pack of Snickers. As she rambled on about her experience in Atlanta, I penciled an "x" beside her name. She wouldn't do at all. She was too fine. So were Kammera, LaShay, and Amber—fine, finer, and finest. I had to find someone unattractive to hire if I was going to keep any help around here.

I stood and shook her hand once the interview was over, gave her the "I'll be in touch" lie, and settled back down in my executive chair. I loosened my tie and released a long, belabored sigh. More interviews tomorrow. I was just about to pray that a homely girl with impeccable organizational and typing skills would show up at my door when my cell phone rang. I recognized the area code but not the number. The call was coming from Arkansas.

My whole body stiffened. The only time I got calls from Arkansas was when my mother, who was suffering from advanced Alzheimer's disease, happened to get ahold of the phone and hit the speed-dial for my number, and even then, she swore I was my daddy, and those conversations were awkward to say the least. If she wasn't whispering sweet nothings to me, she was crying or cussing about some woman she was sure I/my father was with. The only other time I got a call was on my birthday, and that call came from my Aunt Erma. Well, it wasn't my birthday, so it was more than likely my mother who'd probably gotten her hands on someone's phone. And as much as I loved that woman (and I truly did) it was almost too painful for me to speak to her, knowing she had no idea who I was.

"Hello?" I answered softly and a little hesitantly.

"Yes, is this Mr. Ivan Spencer?"

I sat up straight in my seat. That was not my mother's voice nor my aunt's. It was the voice of a young woman, and my interest was involuntarily piqued. "Yes, it is. Who's this?" I asked, putting on my official voice.

"Mr. Spencer, this is Kenesha, your mama's daytime nurse aide. I got your number off of the refrigerator. Look, it's time for me to go home, and the girl who s'posed to come in after me done called in. The company don't have no substitute aide to send for the evening. They been tryna call your daddy, Mr. Wardell, but they can't get him, and he ain't here. I would stay, but I gotta get home."

I felt my head tighten. What the hell was I paying these folks for if they couldn't find a replacement? My mother couldn't be left alone, and they knew that. Up until three years ago, my sister, Imogene, had been staying with Mama and Daddy and taking care of Mama around the clock. Then she decided to go to the casino in Mississippi with some of her church friends and hooked up with a jack-leg preacher. The next thing I knew, she'd run off with him to

Mississippi. She got married and hadn't been home since. I couldn't be mad at her, though. While I left my hometown of Grady, Arkansas at eighteen, Imogene had never been further than twenty miles outside of town up until the time she was thirty-five, when she ran off with her preacher man.

"Um," I said, trying to sound calm since it wasn't this young lady's fault that her boss was incompetent. "Let me see if I can get in touch with someone to come and relieve you. Can I call you back on this number?"

"Sure. Your Mama done hid the house phone. That's why I had to call on my own phone."

"I see. Well, give me a few minutes, and I promise I'll call you back."

"Yessir."

I hung up and dialed my aunt's number. She answered with her usual, "Praise God."

"Hey, Auntie. It's your favorite nephew. How you doing?" I said, trying to sound as sweet as I could.

"Ivan! Boy, is that you? I ain't heard from you in so long! How you doin', baby? Done got married yet?"

I chuckled. "No, ma'am. Look, I was needing to ask you a favor."

"You know there ain't nothin' I won't do for you, baby. What is it?"

"Auntie, can you go sit with Mama this evening? The girl from the agency called in sick."

After a long pause, she said, "Where your daddy at?"

"I don't know, Auntie. The girl that called just said he wasn't there."

"Probably got his sorry ass out somewhere cheating on my poor, senile sister. Son-of-a—"

"Uh, Auntie, can you do it for me? Sit with her? I'd really appreciate it."

"Of course I will. But you know what? You need to come see your mama. She ain't doing well, Ivan. She gettin' worse by the day. The other day I went by there, and she thought I was Imogene."

"Yes, ma'am. I'm planning on doing that."

"Don't plan, baby. *Do it.* I got a feeling time ain't long for her. You need to come spend some time with her fo' she go."

I closed my eyes and nodded. "Yes, ma'am. I am. Thank you so much for doing this."

"No 'thank you' necessary. She my sister. My only living sibling."

"Yes, ma'am."

I ended the call and dialed the nurse aide's number.

"Hello?" she answered.

"Yes, this is Ivan Spencer. My aunt is on her way to relieve you. She should be there shortly. Can you stay with my mom until she gets there? I'm more than willing to compensate you for the extra time."

"Yessir, I can stay."

"Okay, thank you."

"You're welcome."

I hung up and grabbed my jacket. I left my office early that day and tried to dismiss any thoughts of my mother and her demented mind from my own.

3

"Coming Home"

I hit the button to ignore Alma's call again. Damn, could this girl just not get a clue? I thought for sure firing her would send her the message that we were over. But no, she took it to mean that I didn't want to mix business with pleasure and that by firing her, I wanted all pleasure from her. *Wrong*. I mean, I enjoyed that night with her. She was very good at what she did, *all* of what she did. But there was nothing there. I didn't have any feelings for her, and I knew I'd *never* have any feelings for her. I guess I wasn't quite over the whole one-night stand thing after all, and I wasn't as tired as I thought when it came to hitting it and quitting it. And I knew she was just trying to get something from me, anyway. I might have been a fool for a pretty woman, but I knew when someone was trying to use me.

That's why I didn't understand her reaction. She didn't love me. I knew that for a fact. I could feel it. I could see it in her eyes. When she looked at me, she saw a meal ticket. So what was with the marathon calling and showing up at my door? And the crazy text messages she kept sending me in Spanish. I don't even speak Spanish.

I sighed, picked up the remote, and switched the channel from a football game to *Law and Order*. Then I just sat there and stared, my thoughts on my mama. I wanted to call Aunt Erma and see how Mama was doing, but then again, I *didn't* want to call. The whole situation depressed the hell out of me—my mama being out of her mind, my sorry daddy being missing in action. I just didn't want to deal with it. I hadn't been home in over two years. I told myself as long as I kept sending the checks to the agency that took care of Mama, I was doing my part. It was more than my sister was doing.

I closed my eyes and rested my head against the back of my couch. I lifted my feet onto the ottoman and stretched my arms. I was halfway asleep when my cell phone rang again. I was sure it was crazy Alma, so I didn't even bother opening my eyes to check it. It stopped ringing and then almost instantly started up again.

Damn! I thought, *this chick is insane!*

I opened my eyes and snatched my phone from next to me on the couch. When I checked the caller ID, it wasn't Alma. It was the number to my parents' house. I guessed someone had located the phone. "Hello?" I said.

"Ivan! Ivan, it's your auntie. You gon' have to come on home, baby. Your mama got ahold of something done made her real sick. I had to call for an ambulance. Lord, she so sick. She so sick..." Aunt Erma wept into the phone.

"Auntie, is my daddy there yet?"

"No! I don't know where the hell he is. You got to come on home, Ivan. You need to come *now*."

I sighed, shook my head, and tried to slow my heart rate down. Mama was sick? *No, not my mama.* "Okay. I'm gonna catch the next flight out of Atlanta, Auntie. I'll be there as soon as I can."

A few hours later, I headed to the airport, stopping by my office on the way to call the administrative assistant candidates and let them know that I'd have to reschedule their interviews. Then I changed the office voicemail, informing my clients or potential clients that I would be out of town for the next few days. Once I made it to the airport, I called my parents' house to see if my father had made it back home. No answer. I started to call Aunt Erma on her cell phone but decided against it. I was too afraid of what she'd tell me. I guess there are just some things a child is never prepared to hear about their mother. Mama was getting older, but my mind wasn't quite ready to embrace the truth of her mortality—not yet.

The flight was smooth, and I arrived in Little Rock safely and on time. So did my luggage. I rented a car and quickly hit the highway toward Pine Bluff where Mama was hospitalized since Grady didn't have a hospital. It was just too small, barely had a gas station, and it'd been so long since I'd been home, I wouldn't have been surprised if it had been shut down.

I didn't turn on the radio as I made the familiar, forty-minute drive past trees and not much else. The noise in my head would have drowned it out anyway. All I could think about was what condition my mama might be in. That, and where in the hell my father was. You'd think that at seventy plus years old, he'd have slowed down. But no, not my daddy.

After I parked my car in the deck and climbed out, it didn't take me long to make my way through the small hospital to my mother's room. At least she wasn't in ICU. That was a good sign. Once I made it to her closed door, everything in me wanted to turn around and leave, and I probably would've if Aunt Erma hadn't stepped up behind me.

"Ivan? Boy, is that you?" she gushed as she reached up and hugged me.

I kissed her on the cheek and gave her as sincere a smile as I could manage under the circumstances. "Hey, Aunt Erma. Um, how's Mama?"

"She better. I think them pills done worked through her now."

I nodded and tried not to get upset all over again about Mama taking a whole bottle of laxatives. "Well, I guess I better go on in." I grasped the door handle and hesitated. "Aunt Erma, you heard from my daddy?"

"Hell, naw. He probably got his antique behind out chasing some skirt, as usual."

I nodded. It wasn't like I could argue with her, since the thought had already crossed my mind.

"I did talk to your sister, though. She said she wouldn't try to come since you was coming."

Big surprise. "Yes, ma'am."

I turned the handle and stepped inside to see exactly what two years of advanced Alzheimer's disease can do to a person. My mama, who'd always been big boned, was so tiny, and her big, round eyes looked small and tired when they shifted from the blaring TV to my face. The smile she cracked when she saw me was sparsely toothed. And her once soft, almost velvety, chocolate skin was sagging from her face.

"Wardell, baby? Where you been?" she asked.

I shook my head as I walked over to her bedside, leaned over, and pecked her on the forehead. "No, ma'am, Mama. It's me. It's Ivan."

"Wardell, you so crazy. You ain't no Ivan. Ivan ain't but five."

"No, ma'am. I *am* Ivan. I'm forty-one now. Don't you remember?"

I saw a glint in her eyes. "Oh, yeah. Hey, Ivan, baby. I don't know where the hell I am, but the food is terrible. I'd kill for one of your daddy's ribs right about now." I didn't remember my mama cussing when I was growing up, but the onset of Alzheimer's had given her the mouth of a sailor.

I smiled. "I'ma make sure he fixes you some ribs when you get back home."

"Okay, baby. Is you eating? Looking so skinny."

I took a seat in a chair next to the bed. "I'm eating, Mama. How're you feeling?"

"Hungry as hell. Erma, call Wardell. Tell him to bring me some ribs."

"I would if anyone knew where the hell he was," Aunt Erma muttered.

"Mama, you remember where Daddy said he was going when he left yesterday?" I asked.

She frowned and sat there for a moment like she was really mulling over that question, then she looked at me and raised her eyebrows. "Wardell, where you been?! You been sneaking round with that damn Betty Lee again? I swear I'ma slap the taste out that heifer's mouth when I see her!"

I sighed. I was my own daddy again in her eyes. This cycle repeated itself several times until she finally drifted off to sleep later that afternoon. Aunt Erma said she was going to spend the night with Mama because, as she put it, the hospital had good cable, and she could catch all of her shows. I ducked out while Mama was asleep and headed to Grady, to my parents' house, to get some rest.

4

"Good Morning"

Once I got used to the smell of my mama's and daddy's house again, I was able to fall into a pretty restful sleep. It always smelled like a combination of moth balls and chicken grease in that house. At one time, the smell was a comfort to me. Now it just reminded me of a time long gone. My mama hadn't been able to safely cook in years, and Daddy was from the old school. As far as he was concerned, any man that could cook anything other than ribs on a grill was a sissy. I learned to cook out of necessity since any relationship I ever had never lasted, and I'd never been married. But Mama didn't teach me; she wasn't allowed to. I had to learn on my own. I supposed that one of the aides who took care of Mama did the cooking around this place now. Either them or Aunt Erma. But knowing how she felt about my daddy, that wasn't too likely.

Around five the next morning, a damn rooster woke me out of my sleep. Daddy didn't have a rooster or a hen for that matter, so I knew it had to belong to the folks that lived behind our house in a little shack my daddy rented out.

I sat up on the side of the twin bed I'd slept in as a boy, frustrated and sleepy, and stretched. Then I walked the three steps from my room to the only bathroom in the small house and damn near jumped out of my skin. There, sitting on the toilet, was my daddy.

"Daddy! You scared me! When did you get here?"

"How the hell I'm gon' scare you in my own house, sitting on my own toilet? When you get here anyway?"

Daddy had the bathroom lit up. I held my breath as I backed out of the doorway. "I'll wait until you get finished."

"Might be a while. Been eating a lot of pork lately. Got my bowels locked the hell up." He emphasized his statement with a painful sounding grunt.

I thought to myself that it smelled like his bowels had definitely broken out of jail. I nodded, closed the door, and walked through the kitchen and out the back door. My bladder wasn't going to let me wait until he finished unlocking his bowels. I faced the back of the house and relieved myself. I stepped back into the kitchen and looked around, hoping against hope that my folks had a coffeemaker when I knew better. They didn't have a microwave, either, or even a tea pot. So I had to boil water in a sauce pan. I guess I should've been glad they at least had a jar of coffee in the cabinet, even though it looked like it was older than me.

I had just sat down to drink my coffee when Daddy walked into the kitchen wearing a dingy white t-shirt and faded, striped boxers. One look at my daddy and anyone could see why he was so popular with the women. Even at seventy-something, he still had the same smooth, ruddy skin, gray eyes, wavy black hair, and bone structure that made most women swoon. The story had always been that my daddy's daddy's daddy was a full-blooded Quapaw Indian. My grandfather could never confirm this fact, because he never knew his father. But looking at my daddy and the chiseled features I'd inherited from him, I believed the story was pretty close to the truth.

Daddy sat down at the table with a grunt and a sigh.

"Where you been, Daddy?" I asked.

He looked at me for a second. "Here and there."

"Mama's sick. She's in the hospital."

"Yeah, I figured something like that was going on when I saw her bed empty. Plus, you here. You don't come around no more lessin' it's something going on."

I nodded.

I sat there and looked at him and waited for him to show an ounce of concern for the woman who'd borne him two children and had been his wife for the past forty-some-odd years. I waited for him to ask about her or *something*. But he just sat there, grinding his teeth and scratching his head. "Any more hot water? I think I'ma make me some coffee," he finally said.

He didn't wait for me to answer. He stood from his chair with another grunt and checked the pot for himself. Then he pulled a coffee mug from the cabinet and started noisily making himself a cup of coffee, huffing and puffing and grunting the whole time. I cleared my throat and took a deep breath. My face was heating up, but I was determined to keep my composure. Daddy wasn't going to make me lose my cool. Not this time.

"She got ahold of a bottle of laxatives and took all of them," I said.

"Umph," he grunted. "She always gettin' into something."

I took another deep breath. "Yeah, um, the doctor's talking about sending her home this afternoon."

"Umph."

He sat back down across from me and loudly slurped his coffee. So we sat there in silence except for his slurps.

Slurp...

Slurp...

Slurp...

Finally, I stood from the table. "I'ma go take a shower so I can head on up to the hospital to check on Mama. You wanna ride with me?"

Slurp. "Naw, you go 'head on. I'll see her when she come home." *Slurp...*

I sighed. "All right, then, Daddy."

***

I made it to the hospital around noon to find Mama in good spirits. When I walked through the door, she and Aunt Erma were both laughing at something on the TV.

"What's so funny?" I asked as I entered the room and walked over to Aunt Erma to give her a peck on the cheek.

"Ivan! Boy, is that you? When you get in town? Lord, boy, I ain't seen you in so long! Erma, did you know Ivan was here?"

As I bent over and hugged Mama, Aunt Erma said, "Yeah, Versie. He got here yesterday. Don't you remember?"

Mama frowned and shook her head. "Naw, but that don't mean nothing. This old brain don't work like it used to." She reached up and rubbed my cheek, tears in her eyes. "You look good, Ivan. Real good. It's a blessing to see you, baby."

I smiled down at my mama, the only woman I'd always been able to depend on, the first and only woman to truly love me. "It's a blessing to see you, too, Mama." I sat down and held her small hand in mine. "You feeling okay?"

"I feel good, baby. Now that I seen you? I feel real, real good. Never better."

"Imogene called, and your mama got to talk to her, too. It's been a good morning, Ivan," Aunt Erma said.

I squeezed Mama's hand. "I can tell."

I sat there with Mama and Aunt Erma that morning, and it was like old times. We watched TV together, and Mama joked with the nurses that came in and out of the room. She even tried to hook me up with one of them. Mama's taste was on point, too, because that nurse was definitely my type—*fine*. She was a little shorter than me with caramel-colored skin and wide hips. The only problem was that she was married, and though that had never stopped me from stepping to a pretty girl before, Mrs. Nurse was *happily* married. Plus, I reminded myself, I was trying to do better when it came to women.

Around one that afternoon, I was heading back to Mama's room after eating a pretty good lunch in the hospital cafeteria. A short, kind of thick lady with smooth, chocolate skin stopped me as I approached the door to Mama's room.

"Mr. Spencer?" she asked.

I eyed her for a second. She wasn't half-bad looking. *I bet if she put on some make-up and something other than that pantsuit, she'd be a fox,* I thought. "Yes, can I help you?" I asked with a smile.

She dropped her eyes and adjusted her eyeglasses. "Um, I'm Donna Whimper, one of the social workers. I saw where your mom has Alzheimer's, and I wanted you to be aware of the resources that are available for caregivers."

"Oh, well, I'll only be here for a few more days then it's back to Atlanta."

"Atlanta?" she asked with raised eyebrows.

Oh, so you're interested? I eyed her again. Yeah, there was definitely a body underneath those boring clothes. This time, I gave her my country-boy smile. That always got the women. "Yeah, that's where I live, but Arkansas will always be home."

"I see. Well, I'm sure your wife will be glad to have you back home with her. Or is she here in Arkansas with you?"

"Aw, I wish. No wife, no kids. Just a lonely old workaholic."

She smiled. "The women in Atlanta must be crazy."

I shrugged. "It's probably me. I guess I'm just too old fashioned, you know? I like to wine and dine my woman, buy her flowers." I moved a little closer to her. "I like to keep my woman close, protect her. Some women just don't want a man like me."

She looked up at me and even through her thick glasses, I could see the longing in her eyes. There weren't too many women who could resist the earnest country boy act. "Well, those Atlanta women are crazy. I *love* that kind of stuff."

I smiled down at her. "I bet your husband spoils you to death. I sure would."

She giggled. "I don't have a husband."

I stretched my eyes wide. "Come on, now. Are you serious? No, baby, it's the *Arkansas men* who are crazy. I wish… no, never mind. I'm crazy for even thinking this." I shook my head.

She raised her eyebrows. "What are you thinking?"

"Please don't take this the wrong way. I mean, I know this is your place of work and everything but, I was wondering—no, this isn't right." I gave her a sad smile. "You have a job to do, and I'm interrupting you."

She shook her head. "No, no, you're not. What were you going to say?"

"Um, well, do you think you could tell me about those resources... over dinner? Tonight?"

"Yes! I mean, sure, that would be good."

I dropped my shoulders and turned back to the door, trying not to grin as I said, "I understand. I'm sure you don't have the time. A woman like you probably has men approaching her all the time. Forgive me for even asking."

"Mr. Spencer—"

"Ivan."

"Okay... um, Ivan—"

"Can I call you Donna?"

"Um, yes—"

"Well, you have a blessed day, Donna. I won't keep you any longer." I grasped the handle on the door.

"Wait! Um, I said, yes. I'd love to have dinner with you."

I slowly turned to face her. "You did?"

She nodded. "Yes, I did."

I gave her my best look of embarrassment. "Wow, I guess I'm so used to being rejected, I just assumed you said no. Um, can I pick you up around seven, then?"

She smiled. "Sure."

She gave me her number and address, and then I headed into Mama's room. I probably shouldn't have done her like that, but I couldn't resist.

5

"Green Light"

They decided to keep Mama for another night, and Aunt Erma stayed with her while I headed back to the house to get ready for my date with Donna. I almost felt bad about how easy it was to rope her in. But I made up my mind that I wasn't going to sleep with her. I would take her to dinner and maybe get in a kiss or two before dropping her back off at home. I was going to stick to my plan to do better. I didn't want to end up being a geriatric player like my daddy. That mess was just pathetic.

Speaking of Daddy, he was nowhere to be found when I made it home. He was gone, along with his old, ugly, brown Ford truck. I didn't really care. At least I didn't have to hear another round of grunts and slurps.

I took a thirty-minute nap and then got up and showered and dressed for my date. There weren't too many places to choose from in Pine Bluff, where Donna lived, so I decided to drive her to Little Rock and take her to a Japanese steak house. Then, maybe we could catch a movie. *After the movie I'm taking her home*, I reminded myself.

When I made it to her house, I quickly saw that I was right about Ms. Donna Whimper. Dressed in a hip-hugging dress, she was *definitely* fine. Seeing her like that, I wasn't sure if I was going to be able to keep my promise to myself.

She was funny, too. Had me rolling the whole ride to Little Rock.

Dinner was good, and I have to say that I really enjoyed her company. This was the best date I'd been on in a long time. Donna was sweet and smart, had never been married, had no kids, loved her job. She was only twenty-eight and was hoping to settle down soon. She had family ties to Grady, so that gave us a little something in common.

We caught the new Denzel movie after dinner. It was a good flick, but sitting there in the dark next to her got to me. And then, when I laid my hand on her thigh, she didn't protest. Then, when I leaned over and kissed her cheek, she just smiled at me. See, she was sending these signals to me, letting me know she was down.

So after the movie, after we'd climbed into my rental car, I looked over at her and said, "You know, I can't remember when I've ever had such a good time with a woman. You are special, Donna Whimper."

"Same here. You're special, too, Ivan. Very special."

"It gets hard, you know, with my mother's condition. Sometimes I just need to unwind and have fun. You've helped me do that tonight." I leaned in and kissed her softly. "Thank you."

"Thank *you*. You saved me from a night of watching the ID Channel and eating Top Ramen for dinner. This was *much* better."

We both laughed.

Then I put on my serious face. "Would you mind if I gave you a real kiss right now?"

"No, I wouldn't mind at all," she said softly.

I leaned across the center console and kissed her, pulling her to me and holding her tightly. I could feel her press her body into mine and… well, that did it.

"Donna, I want to ask you something," I said after we'd pulled away from each other.

"Yes?" she asked breathily.

"It's been a long time since I've... I've been with a woman, and I just want to be with you right now. I know we just met, and I'll understand if you say no—"

"Okay."

"Really?"

She nodded. "Yeah, *really*."

So I drove to a hotel and got us a room and well, you know.

***

I really felt bad about sleeping with Donna, because I knew what would come next. I knew I was going to lose interest in her, because I always did. Usually, I would spend a couple of months with them, tops—most of the time, not even that long. After that, I just got tired of them. As bad as I wished I could stop, I just couldn't. It was sad, but it was true. Don't ask me why, because I just don't know. That was the way I'd always been. The longest relationship I ever had with a woman was back in high school. I dated Latoya Smith for three straight years. She was the closest thing I'd ever found to Mrs. Roundtree, and I was crazy about her, too. But when I left Grady, I left her behind, hadn't seen her or talked to her since.

That was why none of my relationships ever worked out. I just wasn't made for it. Maybe it was the whorish genes passed down to me from my daddy. Who knows? All I know is, I was relieved to find out they were discharging my mother from the hospital the next day. It was going to be hard to dodge Donna if I was going to have to go to her place of work every day. But that wasn't going to keep her from calling, because I knew she would call. They always did.

6

"Comin' From Where I'm From"

It didn't take long to get Mama settled in at home, and thankfully, the home health agency sent an aide to meet us when we got there. The aide put fresh sheets on her bed and made her dinner and even tucked her in for the night. The only problem I had now was that Daddy was still MIA, and I needed to get back to Atlanta. Aunt Erma had already made it clear that she couldn't stay there all the time with Mama, because she had her own house to tend to. I understood where she was coming from. I had a life in Atlanta. It might not have been exactly the life I was striving for, but it was mine, and I missed it. I'd had enough of the dirt roads and farmland that comprised Grady. I was tired of passing by the same little houses that had lined the same roads since I was a kid. I missed sushi take-out and strip clubs. Hell, I almost missed crazy Alma.

But most of all, I couldn't take another second of watching my mama slide in and out of dementia. There is nothing sadder than watching someone you love fade away. I loved my mama, would do anything for her. I'd go to hell and back with gasoline drawers on if she needed me to. I was strong enough to endure a lot of things. But watching the woman who nurtured and raised me transition into her second childhood was too much. I needed to leave that place, and I knew once I left, I probably wouldn't be back until my mother's funeral. And after that, I probably would never bother coming back at all. There would be no reason to.

So Daddy's little disappearing act really put a hitch in my plans. Someone needed to be in the house with Mama. Yeah, the aides were there, but she had to have a primary caregiver in that house with her, too, since she was incompetent. If I left her alone with those aides, the state would probably take custody of her and place her in a nursing home, and that was the one thing I had always promised myself would never happen. My mother was *never* going into one of those homes. *Never.*

Since Imogene was out of the question, and the rest of my local relatives were just as old as my parents or dead, that left Daddy. *Where the hell was he?*

The next morning after Mama's first night back home, I woke up with a headache, headed to the kitchen, and realized there was no more coffee. I shuffled back to my room, pulled on a dirty pair of jeans and a t-shirt, and told the aide who'd just arrived that I was headed up to the only store in town to see if I could get some decent coffee. All they had was old decaf, but that was just going to have to work for now. I'd head to the IGA in Gould for some real coffee later.

I decided to take a little ride through Grady before heading home. Since I'd been there, all I'd seen was the scenery of the route from the highway down the road to my parents' house. I was riding along, humming with the radio, when I thought I spotted Daddy's old Ford truck parked in front of a light blue, single-wide trailer. I slowed down a little to get a better look at it. I was pretty sure it was Daddy's truck. His raggedy, army green fishing boat was even hitched to the back of it.

I pulled to a stop on the road and stared at the trailer for a moment. The yard was full of dirt and toys—tricycles, trucks, dolls. I frowned and tried to figure out whose trailer it was. Then I sat there and tried to decide whether or not to knock on the door and see if Daddy was in there. Well, I needed to know, and if he was in there, he needed to come home so *I* could go home.

I climbed out of the car and slowly walked toward the trailer. I had to be cautious. Just about everyone in the county owned at least one gun, and some folks would consider what I was doing trespassing. Plus, I had no idea if this was a white person's house or a black person's house. And though times had changed, most racial attitudes hadn't. The fact was, I was a black man knocking on someone's door before ten o'clock in the morning. That alone could give a white man a reason to shoot first and ask questions later. And everyone knows that being unarmed doesn't make a black man any less threatening to some folks than if he were carrying an Uzi.

I knocked and then stepped back a little and waited. After about two minutes, the dingy door groaned open and a little girl, probably no more than six years old, stood before me.

She frowned a little as she looked up at me. "Who you?" she asked.

"Um, can you tell me whose truck that is out there?" I asked, not bothering to answer her question. Even if I had answered it, she still wouldn't have known who I was.

She peered around me and said, "You mean my daddy's truck?"

It was my turn to frown, and then I told myself that that couldn't have been *my* daddy's truck. Not if it was *her* daddy's truck. "Who is your daddy?" I asked.

"Mr. Wardell Spencer."

I stared at the little girl, at her eyes and bone structure and the wavy, unkempt hair that covered her head. As I stood there, a little boy walked up behind her. He looked even younger than the little girl. And he looked just like my daddy. I stood there, frozen, trying to wrap my mind around what was going on. The two kids, my little brother and sister, stared right back at me. Then the little girl turned her head and yelled, "Mama! Somebody here to see Daddy!"

I didn't move a muscle. I *couldn't* move. I was in shock, and I needed to see who this woman was. After a few seconds, a short, okay-looking woman with tired eyes and a scarf covering her hair appeared in the doorway wearing a worn housecoat and dingy house shoes. "Wardell busy. Can I help you?" she asked, looking me up and down.

I stood there and wondered how she couldn't look at me and tell who I was. I looked just like my father except I was a little taller and thinner.

She raised her eyebrows. "Well?"

"Do you know who I am?" I asked, trying to steady my voice, because the thought of my daddy laying up in this dilapidated trailer with this… woman, playing house while my mama was suffering made me want to tear the damn metal off of that trailer and beat my daddy's ass with it. I was mad as hell that *this* was where he'd been disappearing to.

She rolled her eyes. "It's too damn early in the mornin' for this mess. *Should* I know you?"

Right then the little girl reappeared in the doorway with a baby on her hip. I knew it couldn't belong to that little girl, but I sure hoped it didn't belong to that woman and my daddy. Three kids? What the hell?

"My name is Ivan Spencer, and that's my daddy's truck parked out there in your yard. Is he here?"

Her eyes were stretched wide as she backed into the trailer a little bit. "You who?"

"I'm Ivan Lee Spencer. My daddy is Wardell Spencer. He in there? Because if he is, I'ma need him to come see about my mother."

She stumbled as she backed all the way into the trailer and shouted, "Wardell! Wardell! Come to the door!"

About a minute later, I heard my father's voice. "What is it, Ebony? I was tryna watch the damn ball game. Too much yelling going on, and Junior need his diaper changed. Hell, I'm too old for all this yelling and—" He moved into the doorway, looked up and saw me, and stopped dead in his tracks.

"What the hell you doing, Daddy?" I asked as calmly as I could. "Mama's back home, and you're down here?"

He sighed as he leaned against the door. "Look, son, I ain't no use to your mama no more, and she ain't no use to me. I ain't going back to the house. I'ma stay right here with my family."

I frowned and backed away from him. "*Family?* You shacked up down here, in the same damn town! This ain't your family! My mama stood by you all these years and this is how you gon' treat her?!"

He shook his head. "Your mama don't know if I'm there or not. And when I'm there, half the time she don't even know who I am. Don't make no difference now."

"It makes a difference to me! I know who you are, *where* you are! Who gon' stay with Mama if you don't?"

He scratched his head and looked up at me. "I was thinking you could put her in a home. She ain't gon' know one way or another."

"I ain't putting my mama in no home! What is wrong with you?!"

The baby started crying, Daddy glanced into the trailer and back at me. "Keep it down. Junior easily scared. Don't take much to make him cry."

That was it. That did it for me. "Junior?! You are seventy-something damn years old! The hell you doing over here playing house with some woman younger than me?! You really think that young-ass girl wants you, Daddy?" I turned to leave.

"Don't matter. I want her, and she give me everythang I need. Give me what your mama ain't been able to give me in years."

"You son of a—" I stepped off the porch, picked up the tricycle, and threw it at his truck, cracking the windshield. Then I started kicking the truck door, cussing the whole time.

The little boy ran outside and grabbed my leg. "Leave my daddy's truck alone!" he screamed.

"Darnello! Leave that man alone!" my father's baby mama yelled.

I kept kicking and accidentally knocked my daddy's demon seed off of me. I looked down at the little boy lying in the dirt, crying, and then over at my daddy and the rest of his "family" standing on the porch, and I shook my head. "If you don't bring your old tail home to see about my mama, your *wife*, you are dead to me, old man. Believe that."

I walked back to my car and climbed in. Daddy never moved a muscle.

7

"Hard Times"

I was so mad by the time I made it back home, I forgot and left the coffee in the car. I stalked into the house, slamming the door behind me. Then I stalked into my room and slammed that door, too. To be honest, I had no business being that mad at Daddy. It's not like him cheating was a surprise. There had always been rumors spread around town about him having other families. This little family with Ebony was just the latest one. I grew up knowing that I was probably related to half the kids at my school because of Daddy's infidelity. No, I don't think I was really mad about how he was treating my mother. But I was mad as hell at the thought of having to stay in that house, in that town, in that godforsaken state, for another doggone day.

I sat on the side of my bed and clutched my head in my hands and tried to figure out what I was going to do. I had to get out of there. I had to go back home. I had a business to run. I had a livelihood to maintain. I couldn't depend on my business associates to keep running things for me indefinitely. And what about all of the new client contacts I was missing out on? What about all of the money I was losing?

I kicked my shoes off of my feet with such force that they landed on the other side of the room. There had to be something I could do. Maybe Aunt Erma would agree to stay since Daddy wasn't coming back. Yeah, that would work!

I called her, listened as she quickly and kindly refused, and then I slumped back onto my bed. *Back to square one,* I thought. There was only one more option—my sister, Imogene. I walked outside, into the middle of the front yard to call her so that the aide wouldn't hear me cuss her out, because a conversation with my sister almost always ended with one of us cussing the other out.

I dialed the number, held the phone, and wanted to hang up when I heard her say, "Pastor Bishop's residence." She sounded so happy I could spit. I wanted to ask her what he was the pastor of. Their living room?

"Hey, Imogene, It's Ivan. How you doing?"

"Ivan? Well, ain't this something? I ain't talked to you since I moved out and got married. I'm great. Loving married life. How's Mama?"

"She ain't doing too good, Imogene, and Daddy's in the wind, as usual."

"Damn shame Daddy's old behind still creepin'. Lord knows I'm glad I found the good pastor. That man is good to me!"

"Yeah, good for you. Um, look, I'm here with Mama now, but I need to get back home to the A. I can't leave her alone, even with the aides here around the clock. She's got to have a guardian present."

"Hmm, you ask Aunt Erma?"

"Yeah, she says she can't do it."

"Figures. She ain't good for much of nothing except being nosy as hell. Well, you gon' just have to wait til' Daddy comes home, then. He always does. I can't tell you how many disappearing acts he pulled before I left. Used to get on my ever-lovin' nerves!"

"He said he's gone for good. Done shacked up with some young girl and her kids. Got a new baby."

"Umph, I knew it would happen sooner or later. He finally got ahold of something so young and hot he can't let it go. So what you gonna do?"

I closed my eyes and rubbed my forehead. "Well, I was wondering if you could come back for a while and stay with Mama until I figure things out. I mean, I'm the one paying for the help to come in. I need to get back home and get to work so I can *keep* paying for it."

"Ivan, I got a husband and a home to take care of. I can't move back there."

"Imogene, this is Mama I'm talking about. She needs you."

"Mama don't know me from nobody else. Hell, she probably don't know *you*! I'm not leaving my home to come back there and probably get cussed out by her because she thinks I'm one of those heifers Daddy crept around with back in the day. Nope, I ain't gon' do it."

I took a deep breath and tried to calm myself. She sounded just as stupid as Daddy did. "Look, Imogene, Mama probably ain't got too much longer. The doctor said her Alzheimer's is progressing really fast. Don't you think you need to try and spend as much time with her as you can?"

"Don't you need to spend some time with her, too?"

"That's what I'm doing right now."

"And that's what I did for years on top of years. I cooked, I cleaned, I even washed Mama's behind, Ivan. I got my own life now, and I'm not about to drop it and come back there. I'm sorry."

Click.

I just stood there in the middle of the yard in disbelief. Not only had she blown me off, she'd hung up on me. I wanted to call her trifling behind back and cuss her out. No, I wanted to drive to that jack-leg house she shared with that jack-leg husband of hers and beat her down like I used to when we were kids. *Pastor Bishop*, what the hell kind of name was that?

About ten minutes later, I was still standing in the front yard, staring at my phone and trying to figure out what I was going to do about Mama when I noticed a truck on the road, kicking up dirt as it turned into my parents' driveway. As it came closer, I realized it was my father's truck. As mad as I was at him, I was glad to see that the old fool had found his senses again. I was so glad to see him park that truck behind my rental car, I wanted to shout and jump up and down. Instead, I ran up onto the porch and dashed into my room to start packing.

I was only in there for about fifteen minutes when I heard the old truck engine begin to roar again. I rushed through the house to the front porch in time to see Daddy pulling out of the driveway. In the bed of his truck was his old, barrel-style barbeque grill. I stood there and stared at the cloud of dust he left behind for a long time. I was disappointed, but more than that, I was *angry*. Had he really had the nerve to drive back down here just to get a grill? I shook my head as I headed back to my room. I picked up my partially packed suitcase and dropped it on the floor next to my bed. Then I fell onto my bed and closed my eyes.

8

"Used To Love U"

"Ivan? Ivan Spencer?"

The voice of a woman startled me out of a sound sleep. I bolted upright in the bed and squinted my eyes in the darkness. "Yeah?" I said groggily.

"Well, ain't this something? I come back into town, get this job, and run right into you. How've you been?"

I reached over and turned the lamp on, filling the room with yellow light. I stretched and then fixed my eyes on the woman's face. I recognized her instantly. I think my heart skipped a beat or two. She looked good, *really* good. She had barely aged at all. "Latoya?" I asked. But I was sure it was her. I knew I had locked eyes with the only woman I had ever loved besides my mother.

Her red-painted lips spread into a white smile. "Yeah! It's me. I can't believe you even remember me, you being a big star and all."

I chuckled as I looked her up and down—same wide hips and smooth skin. *I bet if she turned around, she'd still have the same round behind, too*, I thought. "Girl, quit that. I ain't been a star in a long time and even then, I was only a medium-sized star. Now, you? *You* were the star." I eyed her again. "And I can see that hasn't changed. Damn, you look good. Shoot, can I have your autograph?"

She giggled. "I see you're still the same crazy Ivan."

I smiled. "Yeah."

We both fell silent and just looked at each other like we were a couple of stupid school kids. Shoot, I felt like I was back in high school again. Sitting there looking at LaToya was bringing back memories of sneaking behind the school for a kiss.

"Hey, what're you doing here?" I asked. Then I realized she was wearing scrubs. Was she there to check on Mama? "You a nurse?" I added.

"I'm your mama's new night aide. I'll be doing the eleven-to-seven shift, be here all night."

"Cool. You need anything?"

"No, you can go back to sleep. I just wanted to speak to you and let you know I was here. When the folks at the agency told me Mrs. Spencer's son was here, I was so tickled. I couldn't believe it. It's so good to see you. How long will you be here?"

"Um, I'm not sure."

"Okay, well, talk to you later."

"Yeah, talk to you later, Toya. Good to see you, too."

She left and I turned the lamp back off and fell back onto my pillow. *Yeah, she's got that same behind, too,* I thought. I fell back to sleep with a grin on my face.

***

Latoya was already gone when I woke up the next morning. I was a little disappointed about not being able to see her again, but then I remembered she'd be back that evening. In the meantime, I needed to figure out what I was going to do about Mama.

I left my room and headed straight to the bathroom where I continued to turn the situation over and over in my mind. My head started to hurt in the short time it took me to empty my bladder, so I decided to stop thinking about things for the time being, at least until after I got some food in me.

I left the bathroom and walked down the short hall to the room my parents used to share. Mama was turned on her side, her naked backside to me as the aide washed her up. I quickly walked down the hall to the kitchen, but seeing my mother's naked behind had killed my appetite, so I took my cell phone and walked out onto the porch. I sat in one of the old, metal lawn chairs and checked my email. There were tons of them from clients and colleagues. I sighed. Checking my email had done nothing but remind me that I needed to get back home and soon.

I peered out at the empty road, my eyes almost automatically shifting towards the direction of my daddy's new home. If I didn't have at least a little sense in my head, I would've driven down there and dragged his geriatric tail up out of there and made him come home to my mama. It didn't make sense for him to be this trifling at his age. No sense at all.

I leaned forward and dropped my head. I just didn't understand why I had to deal with this by myself. I didn't get why my sister and aunt were being so unreasonable. But what I really didn't understand was why my mother had to suffer like this. Why, of all people, did she have to have Alzheimer's Disease?

My mama, Versie Spencer, was the sweetest, kindest person I had ever known. She was always soft-spoken—never raised her voice even when you knew she was upset. She never said a cross word to my father all of the times he came creeping home in the middle of the night. She never confronted him about the women that everyone knew he was cheating with. She just went on cooking and cleaning and taking care of me and Imogene. She never showed my father anything but respect.

Before her mind left her, she never missed a Sunday at Calvary Gospel Church, served on the usher board, and donated a big pan of her fried chicken to the church every time they requested it. She was always praying for other members, and I never one time heard my mother gossip. She was a good woman, one of the best. Why her? Why couldn't my daddy be the one whose mind was gone? I'd toss his butt in a nursing home without hesitation.

I sat out there for a few more minutes before walking to my car, grabbing my coffee, and heading back inside the house. Mama was sitting at the kitchen table eating her breakfast while the aide washed the dishes.

"There's plenty breakfast if you want some, Mr. Spencer," the aide, Carmen, said.

I smiled at her. She was a big girl, probably about 300 pounds, but she had a nice smile and from the looks of what was on Mama's plate, she could burn in the kitchen. So I said, "Thanks. I believe I'll have some."

Carmen set a plate on the table in front of me and as I thanked her, Mama looked up and seemed to notice me sitting across from her for the first time. "Ivan?" she said, sounding confused. "When did you get here?"

I looked over at her, surprised that she recognized me. "I've been here a few days. How you feeling this morning, Mama?"

Her mouth opened into a wide grin, revealing the remnants of some scrambled eggs. "I'm feeling real good since I see you. Come give me some sugar."

I smiled as I walked around the table and then leaned over and hugged my mother. She smelled so good. That hug reminded me of when I was a little boy and how she would hug me when I made it home from school in the afternoons.

She patted my cheek with her hand. "Is you eating? Looking so skinny."

I walked back over to my seat and picked up my fork. "Yes, ma'am. Getting ready to eat right now."

She put her hands on her hips. "Well, quit grinning and eat, then."

Carmen chuckled softly.

I stuck a forkful of eggs in my mouth and said, "Yes, ma'am."

9

"Dreams"

Mama's mind was clear that whole day. We had lunch and dinner together and we actually talked about my life back in Atlanta. We talked about old times and laughed about some of the fights me and Imogene used to get into. We grew up despising each other. Not much had changed in that department.

It was good to be able to spend that time with Mama. It almost felt like she'd never been diagnosed with Alzheimer's, like nothing had changed at all. It reminded me of the few times I had visited home, in the past, after I moved away.

Neither of us mentioned Daddy at all. But then again, when she was in her right mind, she was accustomed to him not being around. I wondered what about old Wardell Spencer made her stick with him all of those years, dealing with his trifling-ness and rampant cheating. I just didn't get it. But the more I thought about it, I'd never really been attracted to anything but good girls, too. And they'd always been attracted to me, despite my ways. Like Latoya. She was definitely a good girl. We dated for a long time before she gave herself to me, and that was only because I was getting ready to leave town. Latoya was kind and considerate, and I'd left her behind like an old shirt. I guess maybe I really couldn't judge Daddy after all.

No, my situation was different. Latoya and I were not married, and I didn't leave her at home, saddled with kids while I ran the streets. She knew where she stood when I left. She knew, because I told her.

"I got to go and try to make something of my life, Toya. I can't stay here. I'll die if I stay here," I'd said.

She dropped her gaze and slowly nodded. "I understand. Will you ever come back? Maybe come back and get me?"

I looked into her eyes and then kissed her softly on those plump lips. "I don't know, Toya. But I love you. Always will."

"I love you, too."

It was on that very night that she gave me her virginity. It was a night I never forgot.

"Ivan!" a voice startled me, yanking me from my stroll down memory lane.

I looked up from my seat on the sofa to see Latoya standing over me. The light from the TV cast a heavenly glow around her face. I smiled at her. "Hey, Toya. It's time for your shift already?"

"Yeah, I just wanted to say hi before I go in there and tend to your mom. I've been calling your name for a good minute. Where were you? 'Cause you sure weren't in this living room."

I shrugged, too embarrassed to admit that I'd been thinking about us—*her*. "Just got a lot on my mind. Hey, you slipped out of here this morning without saying goodbye." I stood to my feet, my six feet of height towering over her petite, 5'3" frame.

I watched as her eyelashes fluttered and her friendly smile transformed into a timid one. "You were sleeping. I didn't wanna bother you."

I looked down at her, moved a little closer. "You could never bother me."

She giggled nervously, just like she used to when we were teenagers. "Um… okay. I'll be sure to say goodbye in the morning, then."

I gave her a lopsided grin. "You do that. Hey, after you get Mama squared away, you wanna have some coffee with me? I wanna hear all about what you've been up to all these years."

She nodded. "Sure. I'd like that."

***

Around 1:00 A.M., Latoya and I sat across from each other at the old wooden table that had sat in the middle of my parents' kitchen since I was a boy. She smiled as she brought the steaming cup to her mouth and took a sip. "This is really good, Ivan."

"Not as good as you look," I said with a grin on my face.

She laughed lightly. "Naw, I know I look older. Life has been hard for some of us, you know, Ivan? Not everyone was able to go off and live their dreams."

I sat back in my chair and cocked my head to the side. "What makes you think my life was so easy? Let me tell you, a lot of pressure goes with chasing a dream, and if you happen to reach even a low level of success, you have to deal with the pressure of holding on to it."

She smirked. "So you had it hard, huh? Well, you sure looked like you were having a good time in all of those magazines—grinning, dancing, always a different girl on your arm. That didn't look bad at all to me."

I raised an eyebrow. "So you saw me in the magazines? You followed my career?"

"Yep. I was proud of you, too. You set out to make it big and you did. For a while, I was strutting around here like my name was Masta T.I.P.—Thuggin' Is Pimpin'! The biggest star in the C.O.M.M. Urban Productions constellation!"

"C.O.M.M. Urban!" I said with a huge grin.

"Chedda On My Mind Urban Productions!" we shouted in unison.

"The hell is going on out there?!" Mama shouted from her room.

Latoya gave me a sheepish look. "I think we woke her up. Let me go check on her."

"Okay," I said as I shook my head. Judging from her tone of voice and the nicely placed expletive, Mama's day of clarity was over.

About twenty minutes later, Latoya rejoined me in the kitchen. "I warmed your coffee up for you," I said as she settled back down in her chair.

"Why, thank you, Ivan." She took a sip of her coffee and asked, "How did you know you'd be a star?"

My eyes widened a little as I leaned forward and fixed them on her face. "How did I know? Well, I *didn't* know, really. The only thing I knew was that I didn't want to live my life wondering 'what if?'"

"But you had to know you were good enough to make it."

I shrugged. "I knew I had skills, if that's what you mean." I shook my head.

"What?" she asked.

"I don't usually like talking about my past career, but this has been fun. Sitting here with you, strolling down memory lane."

She set her mug down and studied me for a moment. "You did it. I mean, you did exactly what you set out to do. Shoot, I'd be talking about it all the time." She sighed. "I wish I had your courage, Ivan."

"You did! Didn't you move away, make a life up north?"

"I didn't make nothing but a mess up north. Married a sorry man, gave him a baby that he hasn't even seen since her second birthday. Worked my knees to the bone in a factory until it shut down. Never got an education. Now look at me—back here in Grady with a twelve-year-old daughter and a grown son who can't seem to keep a job. And he got the nerve to have a doggone baby that he can't take care of."

"Don't be so hard on yourself, Toya. We all do the best we know how at any given point in our lives. My life hasn't been perfect. I've made mistakes, done and said things I wish I could take back."

Silence settled between us.

I cleared my throat. "Um, and I know you ain't really got a grown son and a grandbaby. You can't be a grandmother looking like you look. I don't believe it."

She gave me a small smile. "You better believe I am. My son, Charles, is 22. His little girl, Sequoya, is one, still up north with her mama."

"Charles? Like your brother, Charles? How is he? What's he been up to?"

Sadness clouded her pretty eyes. "My brother, Charles, was killed about a month after you left—car wreck."

"Oh, Toya, I'm so sorry."

She nodded and stood from the table. "Well, these folks ain't paying me to chew the fat with you. Let me get back to your mother. It was nice talking to you, Ivan."

"Same here, Toya."

***

I didn't sleep well that night. My mind was full of the things Latoya had shared with me, her struggles. I felt bad for her. I'd had my own issues to deal with, but they paled in comparison to what Latoya had been through. She was a good girl, seemed to be a good woman. She deserved better than the life she'd described to me. Someone should've given her a good life. Instead, she'd become a black ghetto statistic, and that truly hurt my heart.

And if I wasn't already feeling bad enough, I walked into Mama's room that morning to check on her and was greeted with an onslaught of cuss words that would've made Richard Pryor blush. The morning aide gave me a sympathetic look as I backed out of Mama's room and retreated to my own. I spent most of the day making business calls and answering emails in an attempt to hold on to a business that was suffering in my absence, and while I knew I was doing what was best for my mother, doing what was best wasn't going to pay my office rent, car note, or mortgage.

I skipped lunch and emerged for dinner to find that the aide had fixed enough smothered steak to feed an army, but when I sat down to eat with Mama, she threw her glass of water at me, soaking my face and shirt. "You lying, cheating son of a—"

"Miss Versie! That's your son!" the aide said as she scrambled from her chair and grabbed a roll of paper towel from the kitchen counter. "I'm sorry, Mr. Spencer."

I took the paper towel from her. "No need to be sorry. You didn't do this. My daddy did." I stood from the table. "Uh, if you don't mind, I'ma change my shirt and head out for a bit."

"Yes, sir. Take your time."

I left in my dusty rental and took off toward nowhere in particular. I just needed to get out of that house. My mother's condition was suffocating me.

I guess I wanted to leave that place more than I realized, because I found myself heading toward the highway. I slowed the car to a creep as I passed Daddy's little mobile love nest. I wanted to go in there and blast him for being so damned trifling toward my mama. He should've been the one taking the cussings, not me. He deserved her rage. He deserved to suffer.

I turned onto the highway and headed toward Dumas, where I figured I might be able to find something decent to eat for dinner. Maybe I could even catch a movie or something to help take my mind off of my situation.

I ended up eating off of the buffet at a pizza joint, which didn't help my softening mid-section. I was going to have to figure out a way to get my fitness routine back together. Back home, I ran a couple of miles every morning on my treadmill. But here, all I did was eat a bunch of fried food and worry and sleep. If I kept this up, I was going to start looking all of my forty-one years. I'd always been told I had a baby face, but I was noticing changes in my appearance each day—frown lines and stuff like that. This family situation was really getting to me.

As I drained the soda from my cup and watched as others enjoyed their meals, my mind drifted back to Latoya. I wondered where she was staying and if she was making enough money working as a

CNA to make ends meet. Maybe I could offer to help her. But then I remembered that being in Arkansas was putting a serious kink in my money-making prospects. I was going to be homeless if I didn't find someone to stay with Mama so I could get back to Atlanta ASAP.

I decided to skip the movie and just take it slow driving back home. But Latoya stayed on my mind the entire ride. About halfway home, it finally hit me. I *could* help Latoya. I could hire her to live with Mama full time. The house had enough room for her and her daughter, and if I kept the agency on, she really wouldn't have to do anything but live there. She'd have free room and board plus a salary. It was a win-win situation for both of us!

I floored the accelerator, anxious to get home as soon as I could. I was going to wash up, dress up, and pour on the charm when she came in for her shift. Hell, I'd sleep with her if I had to. Shoot, I'd promise to sleep with her on the regular if that would help her make up her mind. I was willing to do just about anything, short of marrying her, to make sure I could leave that place and go back to my regular life.

I turned on the radio, switched it to an oldies station, and grinned when one of my old songs began to blare from the speakers. I rapped along with my younger voice while bouncing up and down in my seat. I remembered being in the studio in Atlanta recording "Star City Can't See Me" like it was yesterday. Me with my soft, Gumby haircut, red track suit, and black Jordans. I was full of the confidence and bravado of an eighteen-year-old boy. I was ready to conquer the world back then, or at least the world of rap. And I came close to doing just that, real close.

As I pulled onto the bumpy driveway at my parent's home, the sun was fading in the sky, but there was still enough light to see the big, green Cadillac that was sitting right in front of the house. I wondered who it was. Had Latoya come in early, and if so, whose car was she driving? *Oh, damn,* I thought. *She probably has a man.*

Well, that was going to throw a monkey wrench into my plan. Then I asked myself what I was worried about. *I'm Ivan Spencer. I still got it.*

I squared my shoulders as I walked into the house and found myself face to face with my sister, Imogene.

10

"Life Has a Way"

As soon as my feet hit the living room floor and the door slammed into place behind me, Imogene rushed to me and pulled me into a tight hug. She was crying loudly into my shirt while saying something that I couldn't make out. I just stood there for a minute, trying to figure out what in the world was going on. I knew it had to be something bad, *horrible*, because me and Imogene hadn't shared a hug since we were little kids.

The aide was sitting on the sofa giving me a strange look, so I decided to at least act like I held some sympathy for my big, little sister. Imogene had gained at least fifty pounds since I last saw her, and she'd always been on the heavy side anyway. She looked just like Mama.

I lifted my arms and placed my hands on her back, patting it lightly. "It's gon' be all right, Gene," I said softly, but I was sure, pretty unconvincingly. Sympathy had never been my strong suit, but especially not when it came to Imogene Marie Spencer-Bishop or Pastor or whatever her name was supposed to be.

When Imogene finally let go of me and stepped back a little, I could see that her medium brown skin was red and her eyes were swollen. It looked like she'd been crying for hours. I actually felt a little empathy for her. I could see she was hurting. Hell, so was I, though.

Nevertheless, I said, "What's wrong, Gene?" in as sweet a voice as I could manage.

She wiped her eyes and blew out a breath before backing into the couch and plopping down on it. She crossed her legs at the ankle and placed her hands in her lap. "Me and the pastor had a fight. It was bad, Ivan, really bad."

I stood there for a minute and fought the overwhelming urge to ask her if he was cheating on her. I mean, I thought it would be a fair question. Just about every preacher I'd ever heard of was a cheater. Instead, I said, "What happened?" Then I sat in Daddy's old easy chair and stared at her. From the corner of my eye, I saw the CNA ease out of the room.

Imogene took a deep breath. "He found out I've been cheating on him."

I knew it! He's been—wait, what'd she say? "Uh... what'd you say? Did you say you've been cheating on Bishop Pastor?"

"Pastor Bishop."

"Yeah, that's what I said. *You* cheated on *him*?"

She nodded and sniffled. "Things were going so well between us. I mean, we were so happy, Ivan. Church every Sunday. Trips to the casino. We were living the life, you know?"

I nodded, but I still didn't get the whole preacher at the casino thing.

"Well, you know the devil can't stand to see the saints doing good and living right."

Saints?

"So he saw fit to send this fine brother into our lives. I met him at the casino one Saturday. Pastor wasn't there—"

"Um, Imogene, does your husband have a first name?"

She gave me a look that said she thought I was the crazy one for asking that question. "Of course he does." She stared at me blankly.

"Is it Pastor?"

"No."

Awkward Silence.

I blew out a breath. "Uh, okay. You were at the casino..."

She nodded. "Yes, I was there with a group of my female friends. Pastor was at a minister's retreat. Anyway, this fine young man approached me and started complimenting me. I don't know if you can tell, but I've gained a few pounds, so I guess his words really got to me."

"Doesn't your husband compliment you?" That's player rule number one. Didn't Pastor Bishop know that?

"Well, yes, of course he does." She hesitated and then said, "Um, Pastor's older than me."

"Really? How old is he?"

She dipped her head and fixed her eyes on the floor. "Seventy."

I leaned forward. "What?!"

"And he's impotent."

"And he's mad at you for cheating?!"

"I took vows, Ivan, and I broke them."

I rubbed my forehead. "I'm tryna figure out why the hell you took vows with a man old enough to be your daddy."

"Because I love him, and he's a good man. Didn't matter to me about his age or... well, you know."

I shook my head. Was she really that desperate to get married and leave home? I guess she was, and being home for this short period of time, I understood why.

The tears started rolling again. "It's over. He put me out this morning. I didn't have nowhere else to go. I guess I'm stuck here at home again."

I stood and walked over to her. I laid my hand on her shoulder and sighed. "It's gonna be all right, Imogene." *Thank God I can leave now*, I thought.

***

That night, Latoya said, "hi," when she first arrived, and then went about the business of taking care of Mama. She seemed to have something on her mind, and she also seemed that she didn't want to share it, so I left her alone. It was all good since I wasn't going to need her help anyway.

When she left the next morning, I told her I'd be headed back to Atlanta in a couple of days, since Imogene was back. She just nodded and gave me a little smile. "It was good seeing you again, Ivan," she said.

"It was good seeing you, too, Toya," I replied.

But something wasn't right. There was something different about Latoya's countenance. Something was wrong. I shook my head as I watched her back out of the driveway. I didn't have time to worry about her life. I had to get back to my own.

I spent that day booking a flight, packing my bags, and scheduling meetings for when I made it back. I slept like a baby that night, and after bidding Mama (who told me to go to hell) and Imogene farewell, I left my childhood home and headed to the airport.

11

"Better Days"

I put on my best smile as Tracy Johnson strode toward me. I was already seated at our reserved table inside the nearly filled to capacity dining room at Lytle's—one of the newest and most opulent restaurants in Atlanta. Tracy was a prick. That was why he'd made me wait. It made him feel like he was superior to me for me to have to receive him. That was also why he'd invited me to lunch. A lunch invitation is a prick's way of making a business proposition. And because I knew he was a prick, I also knew his offer would be one I would refuse.

"Spencer!" He greeted me as he reached across the table to shake my hand before taking his seat. He eyed the table. "I see you've already ordered your drink."

I nodded. "And my meal." *The most expensive one of the menu, too, you prick.*

The meal was the only real reason I agreed to this meeting. The time I'd spent back home had made me do some serious belt-tightening. I wasn't missing out on a chance to have a good, free meal.

"Good." He summoned the waiter and placed his order. After his glass of white wine was set before him, he began the business end of our little meeting. "Let me get straight to the point, Spencer."

I nodded. "Please do, Johnson."

"I would like to take Spencer Properties off your hands."

I leaned against the back of my chair and folded my hands in my lap. "My company is not for sale, Johnson."

He took a sip of his wine and smiled. "Well, it *should* be. I mean, I didn't mind helping you out when you had to leave town, but a few more instances like that, and you're going to lose your clientele. A lot of your clients were very perturbed when they couldn't reach you. You didn't even have office staff in place to field phone calls in your absence."

I nodded and sat up straight in my seat. "I'm aware of that, but I think they understand now that the circumstances were extreme and beyond my control. Everything has been resolved, and thanks for your concern, but I now have an assistant."

He reached into his briefcase and pulled out a folder. "Here's my proposal. Take it, read over it. Call me if you change your mind. I think you'll find that what I'm offering is very generous."

I took the folder and shook my head. "Thank you for the offer, but there's nothing in this folder that could make me reconsider my decision."

"We shall see," he said with a smirk.

Tracy came from old money, and he was used to getting his way, but this was one battle he was going to lose. I had worked hard to shake my has-been rapper persona to become a respected member of the business world. I wasn't giving my company to him, regardless of the amount of money he was offering.

***

In the two months since I'd returned to my life, the life I was meant to live, I lost a few pounds, gained a few clients, hired an older, unattractive, but seasoned, assistant, and slept with crazy Alma Lopez six times. Okay, I knew better than to open that door again, but what was I supposed to do? Be celibate? Try to find someone to start a real relationship with? Those two options were never going to happen as long as I was in my right mind. I'd accepted that.

I couldn't be celibate. It just was not in my nature. I mean, look at my father. I had inherited genes that required me to have sex on the regular. And the whole real relationship thing? Hell, naw! Who wants to be chained to one person for the rest of their life? I didn't understand how any man could honestly pledge love and devotion to one soul for eternity. It was like something out of a sci-fi movie to me. Like, that stuff would make a good *X-Files* movie if you asked me. I must've been out of my mind when I was thinking about settling down.

At any rate, life was running smoothly. My bank account was returning to its former glory. And from where I sat, my future held nothing but good things.

12

"Another Again"

I was lying in my bed, in my place, with Shay lying next to me. Or was it Sheila? I always got those two mixed up. Anyway, I was lying there asleep, without a care in the world when my phone rang. As soon as I reached for my phone and held it in front of me in the darkness to check the screen, I knew something bad had happened. Something was wrong.

At first I just lay there staring at the screen as my parents' number continued to flash across it. It was three in the morning. Was Mama sick, or worse, *dead*? Was it Daddy? I glanced over at Shay or whoever she was. She hadn't moved a muscle. I refocused on the phone right as it stopped ringing. *No, it wasn't about Daddy,* I thought as the phone resumed ringing. He was too trifling to die.

"You gonna get that?" my bed partner asked with her eyes still tightly shut.

"Yeah," I said as I climbed out of bed, pulled on my underwear, and answered the phone as I walked into the bathroom and shut the door. "Hello?"

"Ivan?" It was Latoya.

"Toya? What's going on? Is my mama okay?"

"She's fine. It's your sister, Imogene."

I sat down on the toilet seat. "Imogene? Something happened to Imogene?"

"Um, I guess something happened, because she just left here with a packed suitcase. Told me I should call you."

"What?! Where'd she go?"

"Home, back to her husband."

"She just upped and left without letting me know what she was planning to do? That's trifling as hell!"

Silence from Latoya.

"I'm sorry for yelling, Toya. This isn't your fault. Look, let me see if I can get in touch with Imogene and call you back."

"Okay. Um… Ivan, my shift is over in four hours. Someone is gonna have to be here with Miss Versie at shift change."

I sighed as I gripped the back of my head. "I know, I know, Toya. Look, thanks for calling me. I'ma call you right back."

"Okay."

I hung up and dialed Imogene's number. "Hello?" she answered in a calm voice.

"Gene, it's Ivan. Where are you?"

"On my way home."

"Now? In the middle of the night?"

"Yes, my husband needs me. He called me and told me he needs me."

Okay, dude was old as dirt, so maybe he was sick or something. I could understand her leaving like that if that was the case. "He's sick?"

"No, he just *needs* me. He missed me. Things are good between us now."

I stood from the toilet. "Imogene, you left Mama in the middle of the night like something was on fire. You know she can't be left alone!"

"She ain't alone. Latoya is there."

"Imogene! The agency won't keep taking care of Mama if there's not a guardian there with her. You *know* that! You need to turn around right now!"

"Naw, I can't do that. My husband needs me. Why don't you call Daddy?"

"You know good and damn well Daddy calls himself done left Mama. What is wrong with you, Imogene? This mess you pulling is trifling as hell!"

She sighed heavily into the phone. "Look, I'm married, Ivan, and my marriage is the most important thing in my life. I can't stay there and take care of Mama. You're just gonna have to do it. I mean, you're the one who's fancy free. No wife or kids."

"But I have a life, Imogene, and it damn sure ain't in Grady!"

"Then maybe we should just put Mama in a home."

My mouth fell open. "I can't believe you just said that, Imogene."

"It's strangers coming into the house taking care of her, anyway. A home won't be much different."

"I ain't putting my mama in no home, Imogene."

"Then I guess you better figure something out, 'cause I ain't turning around."

Click.

I tossed my phone on the floor and let out a low groan. Then I walked back into my bedroom and yanked the covers off of what's her name. She bolted upright in the bed and shrieked, "What are you doing?!"

"You gotta go," I said as I walked over to my desk and logged onto my computer.

"Huh? What's going on?" she asked.

I turned around and looked at the confused, groggy expression on her face and almost felt sorry for her... *almost.*

"Look, Shay, I'm having some family issues, and I've got to leave town in the next few hours. You gon' have to leave now."

"*Sheena.*"

I turned back to the computer. "What?"

"My name is, *Sheena.*"

"Yeah, okay... whatever. I'll call you later, make sure you made it home safely."

Behind me, I could hear her huffing and puffing and cussing under her breath as she put her clothes on. Then she grabbed her keys and said, "Don't bother calling me, you jerk." Then she left my place, slamming the front door behind her.

I shook my head as I booked a flight online and called my assistant. *Here we go again*, I thought.

***

As I pulled into my parents' driveway, I told myself that at least Mama wasn't in the hospital this time, but that still didn't make me feel any better about the fact that I was there when I wanted to be in Atlanta. I climbed out of my rental, grabbed my duffel bag, and ascended the steps. Aunt Erma, who I'd practically had to beg to stay with Mama until I could get there, opened the front door and met me on the porch. She grabbed me, nearly knocking me over.

"Thank God you're here, nephew! It's been rough today! She been cussing me and swatting at me since I got here, thinking I'm Daisy or Maysie or some other heifer your daddy used to tomcat around with."

I followed her into the living room. "Thank you, Auntie. I really appreciate you for staying with her until I could get here." I fought the urge to point out to her that my mother was her sister and not some stranger.

"Mm-hmm." She gathered her purse and slung it over her shoulder. "She all yours now. Good luck."

"Where's her aide? In the room with her?"

Aunt Erma opened the front door and shook her head. "Ain't no aide. The regular girl called in, and they didn't have a replacement for her. You're on your own just like I was."

"What?!" I said as I dropped my bag on the floor. Well, actually, I said, "What the hell?!"

"Yeah, that's what I said when they called. Anyhow, I best get going. Got a whole bushel of peas to shell."

I followed her out onto the porch. "Wait—I can't do this by myself, Auntie. Will you stay and help me, just until Latoya gets here?"

She looked at her watch. "Latoya won't be here for another four hours, and though I love my sister, I can't take another four hours of her blessing me out. Wardell the one need to be here taking that. Not you and not me."

And then she climbed into her nineteen eighty-something Buick and backed out of the driveway. And I just stood there and watched the dust settle and wondered what the hell I was going to do. Mama wore diapers. What if she needed to be changed? What if she went number two and needed to be cleaned? I couldn't do it. There was no way I was going to be able to clean my mother's private parts. No way on Earth, in Heaven, or in hell!

My mind shifted from gear to gear until I finally thought to call Latoya. Maybe I could convince her to come in early if I offered to pay her out of my own pocket. Hell, I'd pay her a million dollars cash if I had it just to work those four extra hours.

I dialed the number she'd written on Mama's refrigerator, and a man answered. "Hello?"

I wondered if it was her son or her man, and then I wondered why I cared if it was her man. "Yeah, um, is Toya in? She takes care of my mother, and I really need to speak with her."

"Naw, she ain't here."

"Oh, okay. Will you have her call Ivan when she gets in?"

"Yeah."

I ended the call, sat down on the sofa, and held my head in my hands. I sat there for twenty minutes before the thought hit me that I should check on Mama. I stepped into her room, and the first thing I saw was my mother, who hadn't walked since she took the laxatives, standing at the foot of her bed, holding onto the rail. I was in such shock that at first I just stood there. Her bed was a hospital bed, and the side rails were still up. *How in the world did she manage to get out of that bed?* I wondered.

I inched towards her and in a soft voice said, "Mama, what you doing out of bed?" I was afraid if I spoke too loudly, I'd startle her and she'd fall.

She looked up at me. There were tears in her eyes. "Ivan? Ivan, that you?"

I moved closer to her and nodded. "Yes, ma'am. You shouldn't be out of bed. Let me help you get back in there."

I let the bedrails down and then grasped her hand. She reached up, wrapped her arms around my neck, and began to cry. "Oh, Ivan. I'm sorry. I'm so sorry."

My Mama used to be a hefty woman, but now I could lift her in my arms with no problem. I hoisted her into the bed and kissed her forehead. "You ain't got nothing to be sorry about, Mama. You're the best Mama in the world."

I pulled the covers over her, and she reached up and patted my cheek with her small hand. "You were always such a good boy. Even after you left, you sent money to take care of us. I'll never forget that."

I smiled down at her. "You took care of me. I'm supposed to take care of you."

She smiled, took my hand and kissed it over and over again. "My Ivan… my Ivan."

I rubbed my hand across her hair. "You hungry, Mama?"

"Yeah, baby. I'm a little hungry."

"I'ma fix you something. Stay in the bed, okay?"

"All right, baby."

I checked the refrigerator, which was almost bare, and ended up fixing Mama some turkey bacon, eggs, and a biscuit for dinner. I told myself I would have to go to the grocery store in the morning. I had just fixed her plate and was taking it to her room when I heard a thud, a crash, and a scream. I rushed into Mama's room to find her lying on the floor.

Adrienne Thompson

13

"Blame Me"

I sat in the waiting room at the hospital with a throbbing head, tired eyes, and an empty stomach. Mama had screamed when I tried to pick her up from the floor, and I knew right away that something was wrong, so I covered her up where she lay, sat on the floor with her, and called for an ambulance. I followed them to the hospital, and after waiting for the doctor to see her, was told that she'd broken her hip and would need surgery.

I called Imogene to let her know and ended up cussing her out when she blamed me for Mama falling. I called Aunt Erma, who was now sitting next to me with a worried and somewhat guilty look on her face. She had, in turn, called some of Mama's church members who promised to put her on the church's prayer list. I should've been grateful for that, I know, but since not a single one of those church folks had stepped foot in Mama's house to visit her or bring her a damn pie or something in my presence, I had little faith in their prayers.

So I sat there waiting for her to get out of surgery, my conscience killing me because I'd let this happen. I felt guilty about her falling, I really did. I just wasn't going to accept the blame from Imogene. She was just as guilty as I was with her trifling, selfish, self-centered—

"Spencer family?" a voice said.

I stood from my seat to face the doctor, a petite black woman wearing scrubs and a warm smile. I shook her extended hand and wondered if she was single. Then I asked myself what the hell was wrong with me. I really did have a problem.

"Yes? I'm Ivan Spencer, Versie Spencer's son." I glanced at my aunt. "This is my mom's sister. How is my mom?"

She nodded at Aunt Erma. "Nice to meet you both. Mrs. Spencer is fine. She came through surgery well. She's in recovery."

I took a deep breath, released it, and felt my headache subside a little. "Good. I'm so glad to hear that."

She smiled at me again. "We'll keep her for a few days and then you have a couple of options for rehab. She can have a physical therapist come into the home for therapy or she can be admitted into a rehab center. I'll have the social worker get with you so you can better weigh the options."

I nodded. "Okay, thank you. Thank you so much."

"I hear you were there with her when she was injured?" she said.

I slowly nodded and dropped my eyes. "Yes, I was."

She rested her hand on my arm. "Don't blame yourself. Slips and falls are common for a woman her age."

I looked up at her. "Thank you."

I met with the social worker, none other than Donna Whimper, a couple of days later. She was cordial and cold at the same time, and she refused to make eye contact with me. I couldn't exactly blame her after my little hit and run episode with her. But at least she got the picture quicker than most other women. She stopped calling me after a week.

She explained to me that Mama couldn't undergo regular physical therapy, because her dementia would more than likely make it impossible for her to follow the physical therapist's directions. But the therapist could teach me how to care for her, like how to transfer her from a bed to a wheelchair and stuff like that.

She also informed me that as Mama's Alzheimer's progressed, incidents like this would become more and more frequent. "If you don't feel you can watch her, you should probably consider admitting her to a nursing home."

I frowned. "I'm not doing that."

She shrugged. "Well, you'll need to do something. If she falls and injures herself again, someone might have to call Adult Protective Services in to investigate."

I stood from the table in the cafeteria where we were meeting. "She fell. I didn't push her. Why would someone need to investigate?"

She settled her gaze on me. "The agency that services your mother is required to report any suspected abuse or neglect. Your mother was obviously unattended when she fell. That *cannot* happen again."

I chuckled softly and shook my head. "Is this about us?"

She gasped. "How dare you! This is my job! It is my job to ensure the safety of my patients."

I sat back down and leaned across the table. "You are threatening me."

"No, I'm not."

"I'm sorry if I hurt you."

She leaned back in her seat; her eyes softened, and a sad expression flashed across her face before her eyes narrowed. "This is not about us. I haven't given you a second thought. Decide what you're going to do to take care of your mother." She slapped her business card onto the table and stood from her chair. "I need to know what you plan to do before she can be discharged."

I watched her leave and then rested my head on the table. The only thought in my head was that I was going to have to get in touch with Latoya ASAP and convince her to move into my parents' home.

***

I stood in the bathroom at my parents' house, toweling off from my morning shower, staring down at my "thing thing," as I used to call it when I was a kid. "Why you always gotta get me in so much trouble?" I asked as if I expected the body part to reply. Then I wrapped the towel around my waist and turned to the mirror. "Or is it your fault?" I asked my face. I shook my head. *Maybe I'm just too good looking for my own good.* I'd once been told that. That I was too good looking.

I rubbed my hands over the stubble on my cheeks, picked up my razor, and dropped it in the sink when I heard the front door slam shut. I was sure I had locked it before I went to bed on the previous night. *Who the hell is that?*

I walked through the house and found the intruder in Mama's room. "Daddy? What you doing here?" I asked, proud that I didn't instantly think to cuss him out.

"I'm looking for my good watch," he said as he rifled through one of the dresser drawers. "Me and the missus are taking the kids to church tomorrow."

I lost my cool in an instant. "Your *missus*, my mama, is in the damn hospital with a broken hip. How about you take your ass on over there to see about her?"

He found the watch and tucked it in his pocket. "Boy, who you talking—"

I stepped up to him. "You! I'm talking to you!"

Daddy actually looked scared. He backed away a little. "You look like you wanna hit me. You wanna hit me, Ivan?"

"Hell yeah I do!"

He stared at me for a few seconds and then said, "You'll understand one day." Then he slid past me.

I turned and followed him with clenched fists. "Understand what? That you're an old trifling ho'? That you spent your life disrespecting and embarrassing my mama with tramp after tramp. Or that after all that, you don't even have the common decency to stand by her side when she needs you? What is it, Daddy? Because I can't see myself understanding any of that in this lifetime!"

Daddy climbed into his ancient truck and rolled down the window. "You'll understand that when something is over, it's just over. I stayed here as long as I could, but ain't no more life for me to live in that house now. I'd rather be dead than spend another day here. I stayed here for years out of obligation. Then that wasn't enough to make me stay no more. I got a right to be happy now."

I just stood there in the yard in nothing but a towel and watched him drive away. How in the world had he turned things around to make it sound like he had done Mama a favor by staying married to her when he was the serial cheater in the equation? I scratched my head and wondered if I was missing something.

After contemplating jumping in my rental and following him to get a better explanation, I stepped back into the house and got dressed. I didn't have time to waste on Daddy. They were talking about discharging Mama in a few days, and I needed to figure out what I was going to do. The agency had assured me that there would be no more hiccups with the staffing of the CNA's and had even offered me a discount for the next month. But I still had to find someone who could stay there with her after I left, because I couldn't move back and leave my real life behind. I'd tried to call Latoya off and on for the past two days to no avail. I'd asked Aunt Erma again and she'd given me every excuse in the book—from her arthritic left knee to her occasional constipation—as reasons why she couldn't help. I'd even called Mama's pastor to see if he could solicit some help from some of the other church members. He'd had about as much success as I had. And Daddy was still obviously not going to be of any help. And I wasn't about to call Imogene. If she said the wrong thing I was liable to jump in my car, drive to her love shack, and kick both her and her jack-leg husband's behinds. My only option was the rehab center, which I had learned was actually a nursing home. Maybe I could put her in there temporarily, just until I could get something else in place for her at home. Or maybe even in Atlanta. But at the moment, I had to do something since Donna Whimper was on my back. I had called and asked that Mama be assigned a new social worker, but I wasn't sure if that was going to keep Donna out of Mama's business. If she really wanted to make life hard for me, she could easily call anonymously and report something, and whether it was true or not, there would be an investigation. I needed to have all of my ducks in a row before that happened.

14

"Baby Girl"

The first thing I noticed when someone finally unlocked the door and let me into Whispering Gardens in Pine Bluff were three unresponsive residents strapped to wheelchairs which had been situated so that they faced a window. The second thing I noticed were the sickening scents of beef stew, urine, and antiseptic as they mingled in my nose. I was to meet with the admissions coordinator, Angel Branscomb. The receptionist greeted me with a warm smile and ushered me into Ms. Branscomb's empty office, which sat right across from the nurse's station. She left the door open, so I had a full view of the nursing home's goings on as I awaited Ms. Branscomb's arrival. *Big mistake.* In the ten minutes I sat there. I watched the nurses as they sat at the desk cackling, paying absolutely no attention to what was happening around them. I watched them not move a muscle as call lights rang off. And the straw that broke the camel's back—I actually witnessed a frail man as he toppled over in his wheelchair. By the time Ms. Branscomb arrived, I was out of my seat and headed toward the door. There was no way I was bringing my mother to that place or any other place like it for that matter.

I climbed into the car, called the agency, and let them know Mama would be home by the weekend, and then I headed to a medical supply store where I bought one of those bed alarms Mama's new hospital social worker had told me about. If Mama tried to get out of bed unassisted, the alarm was supposed to alert me. See, this social worker was actually being helpful rather than slinging veiled threats at me. I'd made the right decision in having Donna Whimper taken off of Mama's case.

After leaving the medical supply store, I went to Walmart and bought one of those video child monitors. That way I could watch her at all times whether a CNA was with her or not. Since her surgery, her appetite had decreased and she seemed to have trouble chewing some of her food, so I bought some nutritional shakes for her, too.

On the way back to the hospital, I called the social worker and let her know I was making preparations to take Mama home and that I would be staying with her until I could hire a full time caregiver. Then I went to my mother's hospital room and held her hand as she slept. I didn't want to be there. I missed my home in Atlanta, and I missed my business. I missed playing racquetball with my buddies and watching ball games at my favorite sports bar. I missed fine dining. I missed sex, and I missed women. But I loved my mama more than anything in the world, and I wasn't putting her in a nursing home. I was never going to do that. So I accepted the fact that I'd be there for a while, but I wouldn't stop trying to find her a caregiver. I'd take my time, though. I wanted to make sure she was well taken care of.

***

I exited my rental and headed into the hospital early the morning my mother was to be discharged. There was a lot on my mind. I'd had to scramble to have a wheelchair ramp installed at Mama's and Daddy's house at the last minute, and I still wasn't sure if the doorways in the house would accommodate her wheelchair. But Mama had lost so much weight since the fall, I was almost certain I would be able to carry her to her bed if need be. The agency had assured me that a CNA would meet us at the house and that they had her fully staffed, but I was still a little worried. I was still shell-shocked from the fall. I wasn't ready to be alone with her yet.

As I stepped onto the elevator and headed to the back, I thought about my last conversation with my assistant. Three of my clients had decided to take their business to another agency. Without my presence and hands-on care, my business was falling apart. All that I had worked for was going to waste, and the bills were piling up. I hated to admit it, but Johnson's offer was beginning to look like my best option. I closed my eyes and leaned against the back wall. When the elevator finally stopped, I checked and saw that I'd arrived at my destination. As I exited, I ran right into a familiar face. "Latoya? What are you doing here?"

She looked up at me with a mixture of shock and sadness in her eyes. "Ivan. Um, I'm here visiting someone." Her voice cracked a little. She boarded the elevator without another word. I followed her.

"Toya, you okay?"

We were the only people on the elevator. Her hand trembled as she pressed the L for the lobby. She shook her head. "No, but it's not your problem."

I moved closer to her, rested my hand on her arm. "Tell me."

She shook her head. "Just got a lot going on right now. How's your mother? I heard she had surgery."

"She's okay, better. I'm taking her home today. Hope to see you at the house later."

"I'll be there. Bills don't stop just because you got stuff going on."

"Tell me about it. Um, did your son tell you I've been trying to get in touch with you? Every time I called he said you weren't home."

"You spoke to Charles?" She sounded alarmed, looked almost afraid.

I frowned slightly as I let my hand drop from her arm. "Well, yeah. He answered the phone when I called. Why? Was I not supposed to speak to him?"

She fanned her hand in front of her face as if waving off my comment. "I was just... he can be a little rude sometimes. It embarrasses me. I didn't raise him to be that way."

I shrugged. "He didn't come off as rude at all."

The elevator stopped and as she stepped through the open doors she said, "Good. See you later, Ivan."

I wanted to follow her, but I needed to take care of my mother. I sighed as I rode back up to Mama's floor. Maybe I could get her to talk later when she came in for her shift that night.

***

Mama was knocked out from the pain medication they gave her shortly before she was discharged, so I had an easy time getting her home, and since the doorways were actually wide enough to accommodate her wheelchair, I was easily able to get her into the house and into her room. I was grateful that the aide was already there waiting for us when we arrived. Once I picked Mama up and put her in her bed, the aide took over and I was able to go to my room and take care of some business with the hopes of saving what was left of Spencer Properties.

By the time Latoya's shift began, I'd already climbed into bed for the night. I was worn out and decided I'd talk to her later when my mind was not in such a fog. I had a lot to talk to her about, not the least of which was my proposition for getting her to move in with Mama. I was fast asleep when I felt someone gently shake me and as soft as the touch was, I nearly jumped straight up out of bed.

"What is it? Is it my mama?" I asked, stumbling to my feet next to the bed in nothing but my boxer briefs.

Latoya eyed me from head to toe. "Um… no, I just wanted to let you know I was here."

I fell back onto my bed and sighed with relief. "Oh, okay."

She glanced around the room and said, "I used to wonder what your room looked like back when we were in school."

I shrugged. "Just like it does now—small and cramped. Only thing missing are the Run DMC and LL Cool J posters."

She nodded and turned to leave.

"Hey… how you doing tonight?" I asked, stopping her in her tracks.

"I'm fine. I can see you are, too." As soon as she said the words, I could see embarrassment crawl across her face.

I sat up on the side of the bed and eyed her with a slight grin on my face. "Well, you damn sho' fine yourself, Toya."

She twisted her hands nervously. "I shouldn't have said that. It was unprofessional. I don't know why I said it."

I stood in front of her and grasped both of her hands. "I hope you said it because you meant it. I know *I* did."

"Ivan…" She pulled her hands from my grasp and left my room. I watched as the door closed behind her and then climbed back into my bed and just lay there. I couldn't go back to sleep. My head was filled with Latoya, the look in her eyes before she left my room. It almost seemed that she still loved me. Did she?

I asked myself why I cared. Years had passed. We'd both lived several lives in the meantime. She had kids, had been with other men. And I'd been with many women—some as good as Latoya, some better. Why in the world was I lying there in my dark bedroom, suddenly in need of a cold shower or a one-night stand? Why had Latoya affected me like that?

Then I thought back to what we were in the past, what we'd meant to each other. I'd loved her. I really had. I have to admit that I missed her for a long time after I left, but my desire and determination to succeed had overridden anything and everything else, including my love for her. But here and now, I felt it again. And it was more than sexual. I mean, I wasn't hard up for sex or anything like that. After all, I'd just been with Mama's surgeon a few days earlier. Oh, yeah. I guess I forgot to mention that. In my defense, *she* came on to *me*. She'd come for her daily rounds late one night when I'd fallen asleep in Mama's hospital room and awakened me so that she could give me an update on Mama's condition. The conversation progressed to me, my life, my job, my marital status. She divulged that she was unhappily married to a boring accountant and invited me to her on-call suite to talk some more, or at least that's what she said. I followed her there and it didn't take long for me to see her true intentions. The next thing I knew, we were going at it right then and there. I'm not proud of my actions, but it happened. And since it happened, it made no sense for me to be lying in bed in the middle of the night, on fire for Latoya Smith.

After a full two hours of torture, I finally managed to fall back to sleep, but it was not a restful sleep. I tossed and turned until I tossed and turned myself right out of bed and onto the floor. I hit the floor with a loud thud and rolled into the dresser. I quickly pushed myself up on my hands, stood to my feet, and rubbed my head. A few seconds later, my door slowly opened and Latoya peeked in. "Everything okay in here? I thought I heard something."

I nodded as I rubbed my elbow. "Yeah, everything's cool."

"Good." She began closing the door but I rushed to it and blocked it with my foot.

"Toya."

She opened the door and gave me a questioning look. "Yes?"

I reached for her, pulled her into my room and into my arms. She didn't resist. She just looked up at me with those huge eyes, looking just as innocent as she had all those years ago. "*Toya*," I whispered. I softly kissed her cheek. She smelled so good, but not like the expensive perfume I was used to smelling on the ladies I kept company with. Latoya smelled like baby powder and cocoa butter, and the scents made my nose tingle, made every part of me stand at attention.

She stared at me for a moment and then wrapped her arms around my neck and leaned in to kiss me. I met her halfway and as our lips locked, I felt my heart race and my hands began to tremble. What was happening to me? I felt like a young boy, a young *inexperienced* boy, and that damn sure wasn't the case. But even in my inexplicable nervousness, the prominent thought in my head was to get her to the bed. It was almost as if I was sick, afflicted with some dreaded disease, and Latoya was the cure. I backed into the bed and slid down onto it, pulling her with me. She didn't resist that either.

I finally ended the kiss and went to work freeing her of her bright yellow scrubs, but before I could pull her top over her head, she grabbed my hand and stopped me. "Don't," she whispered.

"Why?" I asked. I didn't even try to mask the desperation in my voice. I needed her, and I needed her to know I needed her.

She sat up on the side of the bed. "This isn't right. I'm supposed to be watching your mom."

I pointed to the monitor on my bedside table on which we could see Mama lying in bed, fast asleep. "We can watch her from here."

She shook her head. "This isn't right."

I reached up and rubbed her shoulder. "Hold on. Let me show you something."

She nodded hesitantly. "Okay."

I grabbed my phone and quickly tapped the YouTube app. I searched for the song and as it began to play, she smiled. "You remembered," she said softly.

I nodded and stood from the bed, reached for her hand. I pulled her to me and held her close as we danced to "Whatever You Want" by Tony! Toni! Tone! in my small room. It was one of Latoya's favorite songs when we were in high school, and right about then, I was really feeling the lyrics.

I leaned in and kissed her ear, her neck, her mouth as I rubbed my hands up and down her back. I felt an ache deep inside for her, the likes of which I'd never felt before. She felt it, too. She clutched my back as I kissed her; I could feel her tremble against me. "*Toya... baby...*"

And then, she looked into my eyes, stopped dancing, and backed away from me. "I... I can't do this, Ivan. Too much time has passed, and I'm too old to keep doing stupid stuff and making stupid mistakes."

I frowned. "*I* was a stupid mistake? Is that what you're saying?"

She sighed. "I gave myself to you and you left me behind and you never looked back. I made a big mistake trusting you, Ivan. A big mistake that led to other big mistakes. My life has been, and still is, a huge mess and the last thing I need to be doing right now is adding to the mess."

I shook my head. "I'm sorry, Toya, I really am. But us being together doesn't have to be a mess. We're grown now. We just have to be clear about what's going on between us."

She leaned against my bedroom door. "What's going on between us, Ivan?"

"We wanna be with each other. Right here and right now."

"And tomorrow? What will happen then? More sex? And the next day? Every day until you go back to your real life and leave me here? I don't think so, Ivan. Not again."

"I really hurt you, didn't I?"

She frowned. "You're just now realizing it?" She shook her head. "You really have been wrapped up in your own world, haven't you? You have no idea, no idea at all."

"I can make it up to you," I said, thinking of my proposition for her.

"How? By spending a little time with me now and then dumping me again. I don't think so."

I reached for her. "Toya, I care about you. I really do."

"Ivan... I can't."

I stared into her eyes and said something I'd never said to a woman before. "Baby, *please*."

She opened the door and backed out of the room. "Ivan—"

"Toya—"

"Wardell! Wardell, is that you? Where the hell you been?! You dirty, lowdown..."

Mama interrupted, no, she *ended* our conversation. Latoya left without another word. And I slid back into bed, turned off Mama's video monitor, and lay staring at the ceiling for the remainder of the night.

15

"The Truth"

Latoya didn't come to work the next night or the night after that, and she wouldn't answer my calls. The agency was able to send a replacement for her, but that did little to ease my mind. I was worried about her and... I kind of missed her. Had I upset her that much, so much that she couldn't bear to face me? Had I really hurt her that much when I left her behind? Was she still not over me? I shook my head as I sat at the dinner table across from Mama, whose mind was as clear as a bell, thankfully. I told myself that I was being ridiculous. What happened between us had happened over twenty years ago. She had a grown child now. She couldn't possibly still be hurt over me leaving her behind. But what was it she'd said? *"You have no idea, no idea at all."*

I took my last bite of baked chicken and wiped my hands on a piece of paper towel. Then I stood from the table, kissed Mama on the cheek, and let the aide know that I needed to step out for a moment. I jumped in my car and called Aunt Erma on my cell phone. She was always in everyone else's business, so I knew she'd have the information I needed.

"Hello?" she answered after the first ring.

"Hey, Auntie. It's Ivan. How you doing?"

"Hey, baby! I'm all right, I guess. Just suffering with this bursitis is all." I knew she was sharing that information in case I was getting ready to ask her to help with Mama, so I quickly put her at ease and got straight to the point of the phone call.

"I'm sorry to hear that, Auntie. Hey, I was wondering if you know where Latoya Smith is staying. I wanted to pay her a visit."

"Toya? Ain't she Lolly Smith's baby girl?"

"Yes, ma'am," I said as I started my car.

"She staying in her mama's old house, over on Street of Plenty. The blue one with the white trim."

"Okay, thanks, Auntie. I appreciate your help."

I pulled onto the road and made it to Street of Plenty in less than ten minutes. That was one thing about Grady. It was so small, you could make it anywhere in no time. I pulled into the gravel driveway in front of Latoya's house, right behind her burgundy Toyota. Her place was small but neat with azalea bushes blooming in white and pink lining the driveway. There was a faded white resin chair on the tiny porch and a big bushy fern hung from the top of the porch right next to the front door. There was a wheelchair ramp leading from the driveway to the house. I supposed it had been used by her mother before she passed a few months earlier. During a conversation on one of the nights she'd taken care of Mama, Latoya told me her mother had recently died of cancer.

I climbed out of my car and slowly made my way to the house. I had to duck my head to keep from bumping it on the fern. I knocked, waited a few minutes, and knocked again. When the door finally swung open, my eyes widened. Up until that point, I had only seen Latoya in her scrubs. There she stood wearing a tank top that boasted more cleavage than I'd seen in a long time and very short shorts that hugged her hips and displayed her shapely legs. Age had done her well. She was finer than fine!

"Ivan?" she said with a deep frown. "What in the world are you doing here?"

"Uh…" I said as I stared at her legs. *Damn*, I thought. *Just… damn!*

"Ivan Spencer! What are you doing here?!" She no longer sounded surprised. She actually sounded angry.

I looked up at her face and tried to take my mind off of her *everything else.* "Uh… you haven't been coming to work," was all I managed to say.

She leaned against the door facing. "I know that, Ivan."

"And you won't take my calls. What's going on? You mad at me about the other night?"

She sighed. "*Life*. Life is what's going on, Ivan. *My* life. Not everything in my life is about you. I called and quit my job today. I have too much other stuff going on right now."

"But… don't you need to work, I mean, for money?"

She rolled her eyes. "Yeah, but I got other obligations, too. I can't work right now. My… my son is going to have to take up the slack. Look, Ivan… I can't talk to you right now." She moved to close the door.

"Wait! What if I can help you?"

She tilted her head to the side. "Help me how? Help me into your bed?"

I gave her a lopsided grin. "I ain't gonna lie, Toya. Them shorts ain't leaving much to the imagination, so yeah, I'd love to help you into my bed, but that's not what I'm talking about."

She smirked. "That's all you see, isn't it? Someone to have sex with. You don't see me any other way. It's a shame what you did to that social worker."

I frowned. "What?! What are you talking about?"

"Don't act shocked. It's all over town. Donna Whimper's cousin is married to one of my cousins. My cousin said you messed Donna's head up real bad with your little hit-it-and-quit-it episode. You better watch out, too. You know Donna's daddy is a deputy sheriff for this county."

I dropped my eyes and my shoulders sagged and the only thought in my head was, *busted!* I looked at Latoya. "Look, I wouldn't do that to you, Toya."

She gaped at me. "You already have!" Her eyes shifted past me, to the road, and her expression changed. I couldn't really read it, but she didn't look happy at all. "You should leave now, Ivan. Please, just go." Then she slammed the door shut in my face.

I slapped my hand against the door. "Wait. You didn't let me tell you how I can help you!"

"I don't care," said her muffled voice. "Go away!"

I sighed as I turned to descend the wheelchair ramp. It was hot out there, and she was obviously mad at me about something. The past? Donna Whimper? As I made my way to my rental, I noticed a car parked on the side of the road. A young man climbed out. I figured it was her son so I yelled, "I'm getting ready to pull out so you can have this space."

He nodded and made his way up the driveway to my car. As he approached me, I got this odd feeling. His walk and his build reminded me of myself when I was younger. So instead of climbing into my car, I waited. When he finally reached me, he held out his hand and then almost immediately dropped it. There we stood, face-to-face, both of us silent… and shocked.

"Charles?" I finally managed to ask.

He nodded. Then we both shifted our eyes to the house where Latoya stood on the porch staring at us with a look of horror on her face. The young man before me was a carbon copy of me from the skin tone to the hair to the bone structure to the gray eyes I'd always hated as a kid, because I didn't think they matched my brown skin. Those eyes had been an asset with the ladies, though.

He matched me in height, had the same long arms and legs and strong shoulders. He stared at me, first with a curious expression, then his face was clouded with anger. His eyes—*my eyes*—narrowed as he turned and ran back to his vehicle. Latoya finally left the porch and ran after him. "Wait! Charles, wait!" she shouted. Charles started his car and left his mother behind in his dust.

She turned around, slowly made her way to me, and hung her head. "I didn't want you to find out this way, Ivan. I really didn't."

"All these years, Toya," I said softly. "All these years." I shook my head and gazed out at the road and watched the dust settle. Finally, I opened the door and climbed into my car.

"Ivan… Ivan, let me explain."

I shut the door in her face just as she had done to me a few minutes earlier. And I backed out of her driveway as she shouted at me. I drove back to my parents' house in a haze as the realization hit me full force. Latoya's son was *my* son.

16

"Sista Big Bones"

I sat in my rental car outside my parents' house with my head resting against the steering wheel. My heart was racing, and my head felt like it was about to explode. I felt betrayed, angry, and just plain embarrassed. How had it not occurred to me that Latoya's son could be my son? Why would she keep this from me all these years? Was she really that angry with me? Angry enough to keep a secret like this for more than twenty years? How could she not think I deserved to know about Charles? Who else knew? Did the whole town know I had a son before I did? And Charles? Did he know about me all along, and if he did, did he think I was a deadbeat?

I sat up and leaned my head against the back of the car seat. I stared at the house and wondered if Mama knew. Did Latoya tell her way back when? Then I decided that Mama couldn't have known. She was the best woman in the world; there was no way she could know I had a son and not tell me. No way.

But Latoya—how could she? I mean, really... how could she? All those nights she took care of Mama, the times she told me about Charles. She looked me in the eye and talked about him like he wasn't my son—like I didn't have a right to know he was my son. How could she be so cold? Charles was a grown man, and I'd missed out on his entire life, his entire childhood. What she'd done wasn't just cold, it was evil. *Evil.*

I sighed as I closed my eyes and rubbed the tightness across my forehead. I was pretty sure my blood pressure was up, and I didn't even have high blood pressure. If I wasn't out in the middle of nowhere, I would've climbed out of that car and taken off running towards anywhere. But I *was* out in the middle of nowhere and if a damn tick didn't attach himself to me and give me Lyme disease, a damn mosquito would suck me dry. So I pulled the key from the ignition and opened the car door. I would just lock myself in my bedroom and try to figure out my next move. I'd figure out how to be a father to a grown man, and that was only if he'd let me. And I also had to figure out how to deal with the conflicting feelings I was having for Latoya, because as mad as I was at her, a part of me still kind of wanted her and that was just crazy.

As I opened the door and stepped out onto the driveway, another car pulled in behind mine—Latoya's car. I closed the door and watched as she hopped out of her car, still in those barely there shorts and tank top. I scratched my head and willed myself to focus on her face as she approached me.

"Ivan, you need to hear me out."

As soon as the words left her mouth and entered my ears, I felt my anger rise. I threw my keys to the ground and stepped closer to her, towering over her. Her eyes looked frightened which made me even angrier. What gave her the right to be afraid of me? "I *need* to? I don't *need* to do nothing, Toya. The time to talk was—how old is Charles?"

"Twenty-two."

"The time to talk was twenty-two years ago! Of all people, Toya. *Of all people,* I didn't think you'd do something like this!"

She reached for me, grabbed my hands. I snatched them away from her. "Don't touch me, Toya. *Do not touch me.*"

She clasped her hands together and backed away from me. "Okay… uh, will you listen to me? Will you give me a chance to explain?"

"Explain? What is there to explain? You kept this from me for twenty-two years, Toya. How the hell are you gon' explain some mess like this?!"

"You left and I..."

"I didn't leave the planet, Toya! My mama and daddy have lived in the same house for years, since we were kids. They knew how to get in touch with me! How the hell—" I heard the front door creak open and saw the aide standing behind the screen door. "I can't do this right now." I scooped my keys up from the ground and walked to the house.

"Ivan!" I heard Latoya call my name.

I kept walking, entered the house, and slammed the door behind me.

***

I dreamt of Latoya that night. In my dream, we were younger. She was wearing a white dress and holding a bouquet of flowers. She was smiling like she always did when we were in high school. Back then, I could make her smile without even trying. I guess just being with me made her happy. I felt the same way. It made me happy to walk her to class or to just hold her hand. That's why I was willing to wait for her. I loved her, cared too much about her to rush her. And when we were finally together, it felt right... it felt magical. I never forgot her. Never.

The dream reminded me of all of that, and I wondered if maybe she felt the same way. Maybe she'd loved me just as much and had never forgotten how that love felt. Of course she didn't forget. Charles was a constant reminder of me—of us. There was no way she could've forgotten.

She was so happy in that dream. There was a light in her eyes that I remembered from back then, but the light was gone now. I hadn't seen that light in her eyes since I'd been back home. Life had been hard for her; that was obvious. Not the least of those hardships had been raising my son alone, but was that my fault? After all, she could have told me. *She could've told me.*

But why didn't she?

It made no sense that she would keep this from me all this time and deny me a relationship with my only child. Or at least I thought he was my only child. For all I knew, one of the other tons of women I'd slept with might've been hiding a child from me, too. But why would they? Was I that bad of a person? I mean, given the chance, wouldn't I make a good father? After all, I was a much better person than my trifling father. I shook my head at the thought of his geriatric cheating behind. I was nothing like him. *Nothing.*

I rolled over in bed and checked the screen of my cell phone as it began to ring. It was Latoya again. She'd been calling off and on since I saw her the previous afternoon. I ignored the call and turned my phone off. The last thing I wanted to hear was whatever she had to say. There was no way, *no way*, she could explain her actions. No way at all.

I spent most of the morning in bed and finally got up around noon to find that Mama had already eaten lunch and was taking a nap in her bedroom. The day aide said everything was fine and that Mama had been pretty clear mentally that morning. She also said the agency had called to let me know that a new overnight aide would start that evening. After making myself a sandwich, I let the aide know I was going to run some errands and then I showered, dressed, and left. I had no idea where I was going. I had no errands to run, but I knew I had to get out of that house, out of Grady. So I just drove with no destination in mind.

I rode through Gould and Moscow and Tamo and looked at the houses and the people and remembered my childhood. I reminisced about growing up in Grady and walking the dirt roads with my friends. I thought about how Mama would take me and Imogene to church every Sunday and how—before service got started good—I would sneak outside with my buddies and explore the woods surrounding the tiny church. Mama would usher every Sunday, which made it easy for me to sneak out. I'd just wait to see which door she was working, and then I'd sneak out of one of the other ones. I remember how beautiful Mama always looked in her white usher's outfit. I remember the suits she'd make me wear and how dusty they would be by the end of service. Mama would scold me about sneaking out of the church. Sometimes she'd even spank me or have Daddy spank me, which confused me since he never stepped foot in the church, himself. But no matter the punishment, I would still sneak out every Sunday. And she never stopped taking me to church. I guess she just couldn't give up on me. Mama was a good woman from head to toe, and she had a forgiving heart like no one else I'd ever known.

That was why I knew I was doing the right thing in keeping her out of a nursing home. It didn't matter to me who didn't agree with me. Daddy, Imogene, and Aunt Erma could all kiss my butt if they thought I was throwing my mother away. She never threw *me* away. *Never*. And I was pretty sure me and Imogene were the only reasons she stayed with Daddy. She never had to work, and he paid the bills, took care of all of us financially, despite the fact that he was a lousy husband and father. I would make a much better father than him. Sure, I slept around, but I respected my women, unlike him.

As I turned onto a lonely dirt road somewhere in Lincoln County, my mind shifted to Latoya. Not only had she deceived me, but now I couldn't trust her to take care of my mother. Shoot, I couldn't trust her at all. She'd proven herself to be secretive and deceptive. And… and it hurt. It really hurt. I sighed as I spotted a little building on the side of the road with a sign in front of it that read, *Rita's Soul Food*. I wasn't all that hungry, but I was tired of driving, and I wasn't ready to go home, yet. I decided to go inside and order something. If I couldn't finish it, maybe I could get a to-go plate or a doggy bag or something.

I parked my car and walked into the small restaurant that would easily fall into the category of a "hole in the wall." It was dimly lit, and the dining area was filled with old, square wooden tables with t-legs, and the vinyl-covered chairs were a bright, un-natural red. There was a bar with red stools, and as I took a seat at a table by a window, I could hear Johnnie Taylor on the jukebox singing about these last two dollars. I was the only patron in the place, so it only took about three minutes for a slightly heavy-set, older woman wearing a sundress and a matching headscarf to approach me and hand me a menu. She kind of reminded me of my mother.

"Hey, there. I'm Rita. Can I get you something to drink, baby?" She flashed me a smile accented by a gold incisor.

I returned her smile. "You got any beer, Ms. Rita?"

"Mm-hmm. Be right back with a bottle. You take your time with that menu, baby." She sashayed away, and I thought to myself that Rita was probably some hot stuff in her day. With the way she swayed those hips of hers, she no longer reminded me of my mother but of a seasoned lover. You know, the kind that can train a young boy up in the ways of pleasing a woman.

I read over the menu, and when Rita brought me my Bud Light, I ordered some fried pork chops, dirty rice, and collard greens. When she brought me my food, I asked her to sit with me. She told me she'd been running the restaurant as cook and sole proprietor for thirty years, that it had once been very successful, but that most folks had moved away from the country and her business had fallen off as a result.

"You don't get much business these days, huh?" I asked as I took a swig of beer.

Rita wiped sweat from her brow. "Naw, not like I usta'. But every now and then, somebody'll drop in. I do get a lot of folks through here on Sundays, though. You know folk don't wanna cook on Sunday no more."

I smiled and nodded. "Well, you sure can burn, Ms. Rita. These are the best pork chops I've eaten in a long time."

"Hmm, well, thank you. You know what, this is on the house."

I shook my head. "No, ma'am. I couldn't do that. I'ma pay you what I owe you."

She held up a hand. "You the first person to come through here today. Probably be the last. I appreciate you. You can pay me by letting folks know this place is still open."

"I can do that, but I'ma pay you, too." I wiped my hands on a napkin, pulled out my wallet, and handed her a hundred dollar bill. "Keep the change." Yeah, I was going broke, but I felt like helping her out.

She took the money with wide eyes, and as she looked up at me said, "This is one hell of a tip, baby. Thank you."

"Well, you're one hell of a cook and waitress. I'm Ivan, by the way." I held my hand out to her.

She shook my hand and said, "Nice to meet you, Ivan." She stood from the table and smoothed the front of her sundress. "Well, if you need anything else, I'll be back in the kitchen. I got a pie in the oven, and I don't want it to burn."

"Yes, ma'am."

I finished up my meal and sat there for a while, staring at the nothingness outside the window. The record in the jukebox had changed several times, and now Betty Wright was singing "No Pain, No Gain." I looked around the restaurant and noticed the photos that hung on the wall. There was photo after photo of a young woman dressed in sequined dresses or tight pant suits. The pictures were all old, some were even yellowing. But I could easily see that the woman in them was a stone cold fox. *Sexy*, in one word. She was also beautiful. I stood from the table to get a closer look at the pictures. Some were of her alone, others were taken with other people, most of whom I didn't recognize, but the ones I did recognize were stars—big stars. Barry White, Isaac Hayes, The O'Jays—all hugged up with the mystery lady who, upon closer inspection, I realized was Rita. And then the song on the jukebox changed, and a woman with a light voice began to sing about how she was missing her lover:

"My man left me cold and alone

Now I'm walking around like I ain't got no home

Miss his loving, miss his touch

Can't he see that I love him so much?"

I remembered hearing my mama play that song sometimes on a Friday night when she would sit in the living room all alone. God only knew where my daddy was at the time, and me and Imogene were just kids. Mama kept that song in heavy rotation along with anything by Smokey Robinson or Gladys Knight. I walked over to the jukebox, and my eyes widened when I saw the song title and artist: *Rita Holmes, "Missing My Man."* My head jerked around, looking for Rita, and then I remembered she was in the kitchen. I smiled as I thought about how Mama used to say that Rita was the first female star to hail from Lincoln County, Arkansas. I was the first male star. I moved toward the kitchen door I'd seen her disappear through and called her name.

No answer.

But her voice continued to fill the room:

"I miss his kisses, oh, I miss his love…"

I knocked on the kitchen door. "Ms. Rita!"

"Come on in!" she answered.

"It hurts so bad. He was the best man I ever had…"

I walked into the kitchen and stopped dead in my tracks. Ms. Rita was sitting on a table in the middle of the kitchen and she was—as Bernie Mack would put it—"bucket naked." My eyes nearly popped out of my head—not because she was naked, but because, though I knew the woman was at least sixty years old, she was *fine*. I'm talking Halle Berry in *Swordfish* fine. What I'd first called heavy-set, was actually thickness. Ms. Rita was as thick as a stack of IHOP pancakes—small waist, wide hips. I stood there for a minute and tried to catch my breath. There was something exquisite about her body, like it had been sculpted to near perfection, but there were some signs of her age that were evident. Nevertheless, she was attractive, *hot*.

"He knew how to love me like no other man..."

"Um... Ms. Rita? What's going on?"

She stood from the table and slowly sauntered toward me, finally reaching me and sliding her red fingernails down the front of my shirt. "What does it look like?"

She began to unbuckle my belt, and I grabbed her hand. "What about the restaurant?"

She reached up and kissed me. Her lips tasted of hard liquor. "I told you, nobody comes through here."

She kissed me and touched me until I gave in, and right there on the kitchen table, me and Ms. Rita enjoyed a dessert of each other. She was good. I'd actually have to put her in my top ten—right up there with Latoya.

As I pulled my clothes back on and she pulled her sundress over her head, she chuckled.

"What's so funny?" I asked. I knew I had put it on her like I always did. She had no business laughing.

"I remember how I used to think your daddy was the best. Well, you got him beat, Ivan *Spencer*. I think *you* might be the best I've ever had."

I stared at her as her words began to register. "You… you know my daddy? You *slept* with him?"

She laughed a little louder. "Baby, I don't know a woman in this county with a working vagina that *ain't* slept with your daddy." She walked over to me, stood in front of me, and rested her hand on my chest. "I knew you were his son the second you walked through the door. You Spencer men just got this way about you; plus, you the spitting image of him."

I moved her hand. "You slept with my daddy and now *me*? What the hell is wrong with you?!" I felt like throwing up all over that kitchen.

She shrugged. "I heard you were good—maybe even as good as your daddy. I wanted to see for myself. I'ma have to tell everybody they're wrong. Honey, you are *much* better than Wardell. He could learn a thing or two from you."

I backed away from her. "Everybody? You heard about me? What are you talking about?"

"Humph, it's all over the county about how you messed around with Deputy Whimper's girl. She said you were some kind of good between the sheets before you dropped her like a hot potato. Now I know she ain't lying."

I stared at her for a second—speechless. This whole thing with Donna just wouldn't leave me alone. I shook my head and turned on my heels. Bobby "Blue" Bland was on the jukebox telling his woman that he wouldn't treat a dog the way she treated him as I slammed the door behind me. I climbed into my car and kicked up dust as I raced away from Rita's Soul Food.

17

"Since I Seen't You"

I wasn't sure what bothered me more about my encounter with Rita Holmes—the fact that she had used me for some kind of sexual comparison experiment, the fact that she had once slept with my father, or the fact that the whole time I was with her, I was thinking about Latoya. What the hell was wrong with me? And why did I do it with her in the first place? Dang, you'd think I was hard up for sex the way I'd been acting. I shook my head and looked over at Mama who was fast asleep. I'd made it home just as the aides changed shifts. The new night aide was outside taking a cigarette break. I was sitting with Mama until she got back. The aides said she'd been clear all day, and I'd missed it for the most part.

I reached over and softly touched her cheek. "I wish I could talk to you, Mama. I wish I could tell you what's been going on. Maybe you'd be able to help me, to tell me what to do, because I don't have a clue. I got a son that I didn't know about. He's grown, and I'm not sure what I should do now. I wanna know him since he's a part of me, but I don't know if he wants to know *me*. And then there's Toya. I don't know what's going on with her, but I think I like her—like the love kind of like.

"And Daddy?" I sighed. "I don't know what to say about him. I'm sorry he's not here for you. I'm sorry Imogene took off, too." I stared at her, at the rise and fall of her chest. "I'm sorry I let you fall. I'm sorry for leaving home and not turning back."

About that time, the aide reappeared and thanked me for sitting with Mama.

"No thanks necessary. That's my mama. I'd do anything for her."

The aide, who was young—probably only eighteen or nineteen—and attractive, smiled. "I wish more sons were like you. God is gonna bless you for taking such good care of your mama. Man, your wife is a lucky woman."

I returned her smile. "Thank you."

I left Mama's room and headed to mine, shutting and locking my door behind me. I knew women well enough to know that that aide's smile meant she was interested in me. And if the smile wasn't enough, there was that little comment about my "wife." Any other time, I would've jumped at the chance to get with a cute little thing like her, but my encounter with Rita Holmes had sobered me a little. And besides, I'd used my last condom on Rita.

***

The next morning, I decided I was going to have to get in a workout one way or another. I could tell I was gaining weight again from the way my pants were starting to fit. At that point, my appearance was all I had left, and I needed to hold on to it. So I woke up early, pulled on a pair of shorts, a t-shirt, and my sneakers, and headed out to run the roads of Grady. It was early enough that the summer sun wasn't leaning on me like an overdue bill, and I figured the mosquitos and ticks would have a hard time attaching themselves to a moving target.

I ran from my parents' house and headed east. I'd make a loop at where the old Henson farm used to be and then head back home and have breakfast before spending the rest of the day making calls and sending emails in an attempt to revive my business, which was on its last leg and in need of life support.

I ran past several houses that were boarded up or falling in— houses where lots of my childhood friends had once lived, houses where I'd visited them. I ran past the woods I used to explore as a boy. I ran past Mama's old church and remembered the good times I used to have there as a boy. The run brought up a sense of nostalgia, while at the same time, making me feel a little sad. Everything had changed, and my home town seemed to be dying a slow, painful death.

I was trotting back home when a truck pulled up beside me, kicking up dirt around me. "Well, I'll be!" the driver said as he pulled to a stop. "If it ain't *the* Ivan Spencer!"

I stopped in my tracks. The voice sounded familiar, but I couldn't quite place it. I peered into the open window of the black pick-up truck and grinned. Years had added maturity to his baby face, but I would know that grin anywhere. "Earl Rayford?!" I said with a big smile on my face. Earl had been one of my best friends from elementary school through high school.

He climbed out of his truck, and met me on the road. He was still about a foot shorter than me, but the baby fat was gone, and standing before me was a man in his forties with a goatee and the muscular build of an athlete. He took my outstretched hand and pulled me onto a brother hug. We patted each other on the back and then backed away from each other.

"Man! I heard you were here! Glad I ran into you!"

I nodded. "Yeah, man. Me, too."

"I heard you were here seeing about your mom. I been meaning to get by there. How is she?"

I shrugged. "As well as she can be, I guess. She's got Alzheimer's."

"Aw, man. I hate to hear that. My wife's dad had that before he passed."

With raised eyebrows, I asked, "Wife? You hitched?"

He chuckled. "I'm forty-one. Most men our age are hitched, man."

I chuckled lightly. "Yeah, I guess you're right."

"Not you, huh? Still ain't found Mrs. Right?"

"Hell, I ain't been looking for her. Been busy running my business... and running the streets." I gave him a grin and a nudge.

He shook his head. "Just like your pops, huh?"

I dropped the grin, gave him a serious look. "Naw, man. Don't put me in the category with him. I ain't *nothing* like that man."

Earl raised both of his hands and backed away a little. "My bad, man. Didn't mean to hit a nerve. Hey, I wanna catch up with you, but not out here on the road. What're you doing for dinner tonight?"

"Not a thing, man."

"Come have dinner with me and my family. We live right up the road."

"Can your wife burn?"

"Of course she can! You think I'd marry a woman who couldn't cook? You know how I like to grub!"

I laughed. "Yeah, I remember you could eat back in the day. But you done slimmed down, man. I thought maybe the missus was starving you or something."

He shook his head. "Naw, Tammy can cook, I just have sense enough to exercise now."

I frowned slightly. "Tammy? Tammy Roundtree? Mrs. Roundtree's daughter?"

Earl grinned. "Yep, the one and only. We've been married for fifteen years, now."

I just stood there with my mouth hung open for a minute. No one, and I mean, *no one* could get to Tammy back in high school. She was pretty, all right, but the way she rejected guys, you would've thought she was the finest girl in the school. That title belonged to Latoya—hands down. It wasn't Tammy's looks or her body that made the guys want her. It was the fact that Mrs. Roundtree was her mother. We figured the apple couldn't roll too far from the fine tree. Surely Tammy would end up being just as fine as her mother, eventually. At least that's what I thought. "How'd you manage that?" I finally asked.

"Have dinner with us, and I'll tell you."

I nodded. I wouldn't mind seeing how Tammy turned out or hearing the story of how Earl won her hand. "Okay. What's your address? You say you're up the road?"

"Tell you what. I'll come pick you up. That way I can see your mama, too."

"All right, see you this evening, man."

***

I sat in the passenger seat of Earl's Chevy pick-up and tapped my fingers to the Bobbie Brooks CD that was flowing from the speakers. Bobbie was one of my favorite artists, and I was feeling kind of mellow, riding with my old buddy, glad to be out of the house for a while. Maybe I could clear my head and bend Earl's ear a little—get his take on this whole thing with Latoya. When Earl pulled off of the road into a gravel driveway, I smiled. He lived in a nice, two-story frame house with a huge porch which was cluttered with tricycles and other colorful toys. He pulled to a stop next to an SUV. It looked like my old friend had done well for himself.

"This is nice, man," I said as I hopped out of his truck and followed him to the front of the house.

Earl smiled as he opened the front door. "Thanks, man. We're proud of it."

I walked inside the house and smiled when I saw Tammy standing in the entryway looking just as she had in high school, except for her stomach. She looked very pregnant as she walked over to me, hugged me, and softly kissed my cheek. "It's so good to see you, Ivan," she said.

I grasped her hand. "Good to see you, too, Tammy. You still look like you belong in high school."

"Aren't you sweet? Well, I can definitely say the same for you."

I glanced at Earl. "You and Earl both look really good."

Earl smiled at me, but before he could respond, three little kids ran into the entryway—two boys and a little girl. Earl picked up the little girl and said, "Ivan, meet the crew. This is Nisha. And then there's Earl Jr. and Kobe. Our little stair steps."

Tammy patted her stomach. "And number four is still in the oven. Got two months to go."

I rocked back on my heels. "Wow, you guys have been busy." Those were some cute kids, and Earl and Tammy looked happy enough, but I still didn't get the whole commitment-marriage-having kids thing. I probably never would.

"Yeah, four kids in six years. After Tammy finished grad school, we started working on the kids and we haven't stopped," Earl said as he led me into the dining room.

"Really? How long did you say you two've been together?"

"Married fifteen years last month. Ran into her at a jazz bar in Little Rock one night, we talked until the sun came up, and we've been together ever since."

"Fifteen years! Congrats, man. I haven't been in a relationship for as long as fifteen months since high school. I don't know how guys like you do it. Hell, it's commendable."

"It's easy when you're with the right woman. Tammy's the one for me. My soul mate."

I didn't believe in soul mates, either. "Well, I'm glad you two are happy."

Earl patted my arm as we both sat down at the table. Tammy had taken the kids to wash their hands. "You've got a soul mate out there, too, man," he said. "You just gotta keep your eyes open so you can see her."

I shook my head. "Naw, I'm good. The last thing I need to add to my list of problems is a wife and some kids."

Earl gave me an odd look but didn't respond. After Tammy and the kids were seated at the table, Earl said grace and we all dug in.

Over dinner, I asked about Mrs. Roundtree, Tammy's mom. I found out she'd moved to Florida with her second husband. She wasn't Mrs. Roundtree anymore, and judging from the picture Tammy showed me, she didn't look like Mrs. Roundtree anymore, either. She'd gained weight, and she looked every bit of her sixty some odd years of age. My fantasy Mrs. Roundtree was long gone, and I have to admit that I was a little disappointed. I guess in my mind, I expected her to look just as she had all those years ago.

After dinner—pot roast, mashed potatoes, and English peas— Tammy undertook the task of getting the kids ready for bed while I helped Earl clean up the dining room.

"Man, I'm full as a tick! I'ma have to run an extra mile tomorrow to keep that dinner from sticking to me," I said as I stretched my arms and yawned.

Earl grinned. "Got that 'itis,' huh? Yeah, Tammy can burn, for sure. I can't miss a day in the gym, or I'll be looking like 'little Earl the squirrel' again—fat cheeks and all."

"Aw, man! I forgot we used to call you that!" I howled.

"Yeah, well, I ain't forgot. Man, y'all *stayed* jonin' me. I couldn't catch a break!"

I chuckled. "Aw, man, it was all in love, and we had some good times, right, *squirrel*?" I held my fist out and waited for him to give me some dap.

He bumped my fist with his and grinned. "Yeah, we did."

After we finished cleaning the table, I leaned against the kitchen counter while Earl loaded the dishwasher. "Toya's in town," I said out of the blue. I don't even know why I said it. I guess the situation with her and Charles was weighing on my mind.

"Yeah, I know. She goes to my church."

"Really?" I cleared my throat. "You seen her son?" If he had, then he knew what I knew.

He looked up at me and shook his head. "Nah, I've never met him. The way Toya talks about him, he kinda does his own thing. I get the impression that he's a little troubled. Why?"

I sighed and shook my head. "I really don't wanna get into it right now."

Earl shut the dishwasher and walked over to the refrigerator. He opened it, grabbed two beers, and handed me one. "Come with me."

I followed him out to a screened-in back porch where we sat at a small table. I chugged my beer, and Earl stared at me for a second, then said, "I know we haven't been in touch since high school, but you're still my friend, man—always will be. Something's on your mind, I'm here to listen, and it won't go any further. I'm not one of those gossiping dudes."

I gripped the beer bottle and scratched the back of my head. "Okay... uh, well... Toya's son is my son, and I just found out the other day."

He frowned. "What?"

"Toya's son is *my* son. He's twenty-two, Earl, and she never told me. Never said a word in twenty-two years."

Earl leaned forward. "Uh, I thought you and her never did it back then. I mean, isn't that what you told me?"

"Yeah, and it was the truth. We didn't do it until right before I left." I shook my head. "I know he's mine. Hell, looking at him is like looking in a mirror."

Earl leaned back in his chair. "That's tough, man. Twenty-two years? I can't believe Toya would keep this from you. She's a good person. I mean, she's such a good mother to her little girl..."

"Yeah, well, she *did* keep it from me. Now I just don't know what to do. Do I try to build some kind of relationship with him? Do I just leave him alone? He probably hates me. I know I would. Shoot, I hate my father, and I've known him all my life."

"Did she say why she kept it from you?"

"No, she tried to explain, but I wasn't tryna hear it. I got too much to deal with—my mama, my sorry daddy. I can't listen to no lame excuses from her right now." Earl had visited with Mama, who thought he was her long-dead brother Clarence (yeah, the confusion was back) when he came to pick me up. And I'd told him about Daddy when he asked where he was as we left my folks' house.

Earl shook his head in silence; then he looked up at me. "I ever tell you what I do for a living now?"

I frowned and tried to figure out what his occupation had to do with my dilemma. "Naw, I mean, Tammy said she's a high school principal, right? You didn't tell me what you do."

"I'm a pastor. *Toya's* pastor. I know her heart. She has to have a good reason for keeping this from you."

"You're a pastor?! Man, I been cussing and stuff and you a da— doggone preacher?"

"Yeah, I noticed that cussing. Look, you need to talk to her, hear her out. Give her a chance to explain."

I leaned forward and rested my elbows on the table. "I don't know, man. I just don't think I can look her in the face right now. To be honest with you, I'm pretty pis—mad at her."

"I see your side of it, Ivan. But your side isn't the only side. You owe it to yourself and your son to find out why she's been keeping this from you."

I sat back in my chair and stared out at the field behind Earl's house. He was right, but I wasn't ready to concede.

"Hey, can I pray for you, man?" I looked at my friend and slowly nodded. I didn't think prayer would help things, but I didn't guess it would hurt them either.

18

"Just Don't Have A Clue"

I didn't sleep at all that night as Earl's words kept echoing in my head. He was right. I needed to get to the bottom of things. I needed to hear Latoya out. At least maybe then there would be one burden lifted off of me. And who knows? Maybe Charles and I would end up being close. After all, he was my only child, and I definitely wasn't planning on making any more kids. That's why I was standing at Latoya's door at 8:00 A.M. in the already hot summer air. I wanted—no—I *needed* to hear what she had to say.

She opened the door wearing a bathrobe and a worn expression on her pretty face. Worry lines creased her forehead, and when she looked up at me, there were tears in her eyes. She leaned her head against the door frame, and the sunlight shone on her face, giving her a divine appearance. Her full lips quivered as she spoke. "I can't this morning, Ivan. You're gonna have to choose another day to come and cuss me out or call me names or whatever you're here for. I can't deal with it this morning. I'm just too tired."

I shook my head and tried to speak in a calm voice. "I'm not here for any of that, Toya. I just want some kind of explanation. I need to know why you would keep something like this from me."

She sighed, glanced back into her house, and said, "Wait a minute." She closed the door in my face, and I just stood there and looked around. I noticed that Charles's car wasn't there and figured that was probably a good thing. I needed to hear what Latoya had to say before I decided how to approach him. I needed to know exactly what she'd told him about me, if anything. The door finally opened again about ten minutes later. Latoya was dressed in a pair of scrub pants and a wrinkled t-shirt now. I was dripping in sweat when I entered her small, clean living room.

"You want a cup of water?" she asked.

"Yeah, that'd be good. Thank you."

She walked into the kitchen, which was sort of combined with the living room, and returned with a mason jar of ice water and a paper towel. I rubbed the paper towel around the outside of the jar to soak up some of the cool condensation and wiped my forehead with it. Then I took a big gulp of water. "Thank you," I finally said once I had cooled off.

She nodded.

I looked over at her, at the look she wore on her face that reminded me of that night—the night we made Charles, and I tried to soften my own expression a little. She looked so frightened and vulnerable; I almost felt sorry for her. *Almost.* "The other day, you asked me to hear you out. I should've listened to what you had to say, but I was upset, you know?"

She dropped her eyes. "That's understandable." She crossed her legs at the ankle and released a breath. "I've been praying about how to tell you about Charles since I first saw you at your mom's house. I knew you had a right to know, but I just didn't know what to say or how to say it… or when to say it."

"You've had twenty-two years to figure it out."

"I know. There's no excuse for what I've done, especially to Charles. But I honestly didn't see any other way, Ivan. I was young and alone. Things weren't easy for me back then." She shook her head. "They still aren't."

A loud beep went off before I could respond. Latoya hopped up from her chair. "Let me silence that alarm," she said.

I nodded and watched her walked down a narrow hallway to a room in the back of the house. When she returned a couple of minutes later, she looked even more tired than before.

"Look, Toya," I began. "I appreciate the fact that life hasn't been easy for you, but don't you think it's partially your fault for keeping this a secret. Charles has an entire side of his family that he knows nothing about—a side of the family that would've been glad to help with him. *You* made things hard on *yourself.*"

"I didn't see any other way under the circumstances."

I leaned forward with a deep frown on my face. "You don't see that I would've helped you? Why in the world did you think I wouldn't? What kind of person do you think I am?"

She leaned forward and gave me a frown that I'm sure matched mine. "I think you're the kind of person who would tell a girl you love her, take her virginity, and then leave her behind without a second thought—you know, the kind of man who only thinks of himself."

I stood to my feet and raised my voice a little without trying. "What the hell does what happened between us have to do with my son!"

Latoya fell against the back of her seat. "Your s—"

The front door flew open and Charles stormed into the house. "Yeah, I thought that was him when I saw that car outside. What the hell is he doing here?!" he shouted.

"Mama! What's going on?!" A child's voice yelled from the back of the house.

"Nothing, Asia! Go back to sleep, baby!" Toya shouted, then she turned to Charles. "He's here to talk."

Charles looked me up and down. "Talk about *what*?"

I moved toward him a little. He backed away and held his hands up. "Talk about *what*?" he repeated.

"I want to talk about you and me. I want to get to know you," I said.

Charles shook his head. "I ain't known you all my life. The hell I need to know you for now?"

"Charles, he just wants to get to know you. Don't be like that," Latoya interjected.

"I'm twenty-two years old. What? You gon' teach me how to ride bikes, catch baseballs with me? Tell me all about the birds and the bees like a good big brother? I ain't tryna hear what you got to say, man! You and your family ain't never been there for me. Why start now?"

Latoya stood to her feet and placed her hand on his arm. "Charles—"

"Wait," I said. "What did you mean when you said 'big brother?'"

"What'd it sound like? You slow or something?" Charles asked.

I shifted my eyes from him to Latoya. "What is he talking about, Toya?"

"Ivan," she said softly. "Charles is your brother. Did you think—"

"*Brother?* How is he my brother?"

She eased back down into her chair, her eyes glued to me. "You and Charles have the same father."

19

"Caught Up"

I fell back onto the sofa as the impact of Latoya's words hit me. Charles wasn't my son. He was my brother, my father's son. I raised my eyes from the floor to the other side of the room where Charles and Latoya were talking to me or to each other. I couldn't really tell, because I couldn't hear them. There were too many thoughts in my head, and there was too much anger inside of me, fighting and raging to break out. Charles was my father's son. Latoya had slept with my father. My father had slept with Latoya—possibly around the same time she slept with me.

My stomach lurched, threatened to reintroduce that jar of water to the world. I gripped it and looked up at Latoya who now stood alone by the door. Charles was gone. I had no idea where he was or when he left. "You had sex with my daddy?" I asked in a voice so hollow, I almost wondered if someone else was talking.

Latoya nodded. Tears were streaming down her face. "I was so ashamed of what I did. I felt so bad about it. I still do."

"How? How... how did it happen? Was it before I left?"

She vigorously shook her head. "No... no, it was after you left. I missed you from the second you left Grady, Ivan. I missed you something awful."

I tilted my head to the side. "That's why you had sex with my daddy? Because you missed me?"

She wiped her wet face and released a ragged sigh. "No, that's not why."

"Then why, Toya? *Why?*"

She leaned forward and covered her face with her hands. "I missed you so much. I waited for a call or a letter or something. I went to your house every week to see if they'd heard from you or if you'd sent a letter to me there. Week after week, nothing. You hurt me, Ivan. Broke my heart."

I dropped my gaze. "I'm sorry."

"And then my brother died, and you know we were so close and I missed him... and I missed you, too. I was so lonely. So lonely..."

"Toya..."

"Every week that summer I would go to your house and ask about you. Nothing... *nothing*. Sometimes your mom would meet me at the door, and sometimes your dad would.

"You know I didn't have a car, so I would walk all the way from my mom's house to your folks' house. The first couple of times your dad offered me a ride home, I said no. Then, one day, I took him up on his offer. He was nice to me, told me I was too pretty to be worried about you. The third time he gave me a ride home, he kissed me."

She looked up at me. "Ivan, your dad had this way about him... this swag, and it didn't help that I was missing you so badly, and you and him look just alike. So one of the days when he drove me home, he asked me if I was hungry and offered to get me something to eat. We ended up in Dumas. He got me a big burger and a milkshake, and as we sat in the parking lot at the burger joint and ate, he put his hand on my thigh and told me he knew how to make me forget you. Ivan, I'm not trying to make excuses, but I was young and lonely, and I felt like a fool for losing my virginity to someone who obviously didn't care about me. So I just smiled at him and nodded.

"We ended up at some raggedy motor inn in Dumas, and we had sex. We did it a couple more times after that, but it never felt right to be with him, so I just stopped going around their place. That was August of that year. In October was when I realized I was pregnant. I knew it had to be his because of the timing, since me and you were together in May of that year."

I felt my anger rising to a dangerous level—the level where I wanted to punch something, *anything,* until my knuckles began to bleed. I stared at her for a full five minutes before I said, "Did my mama know about this? Does my daddy know about Charles?"

She nodded. "They both know. When my mama found out I was pregnant, she took me over there and blasted your daddy right in front of your mama. Your daddy laughed in her face and told her to get off his property before he got his shotgun and sent her to an early grave. After that, my mama sent me up north. She said that would be better than staying in Grady and being the talk of the town, so I moved up there with my Aunt May and her husband, and I never looked back.

"Toya, why the hell would you come into my mama's house and play nursemaid to her knowing she knew about you and my father? Why would you disrespect her like that?" I asked through clenched teeth.

She sighed deeply. "Because I needed a job, Ivan. Because I have a child to take care of and no education other than a CNA license I got when I first moved back to Arkansas, and that was the only job I could get. And I'd heard she had dementia, so I figured she wouldn't remember me. And she didn't at first."

"At first?"

She gave me a sheepish expression. "That night we almost—*you know*—she remembered me. Called me everything but a child of God, asked me where my bastard child was. I thought for sure you heard her on the monitor."

I slowly shook my head. "No, I think I turned it off that night. You had me all twisted up in the head. I didn't want to look at that monitor and see you... and wanna be with you."

I could see her blush a little. "Well, that's why I quit. I know I deserved to hear every word, but I couldn't take any more of it. I just couldn't."

I nodded as I slowly stood to my feet.

Latoya looked up at me with wet eyes. "I'm sorry, Ivan. You don't know how hard I prayed for Charles to be yours when I first found out I was pregnant, but it just didn't add up that way. I'm so sorry."

I nodded again, and then I left.

20

"So Gone"

"Open this damn door!" I shouted as I pounded my fist against the raggedy screen door that was locked despite the fact that the screen was ripped from top to bottom. "Open it now!" I stumbled a little but caught myself before falling. I'd paid a visit to WC Green, the local bootlegger, and had been drinking for most of the evening. Now I was standing on the front porch of my father's love nest. I wanted answers, and I wasn't leaving until I had them, until he explained why he was such a miserable, low-down—

"Who is it?!" a voice shouted from inside the trailer. No doubt it was his side piece.

"It's Ivan Spencer, *trick*! Tell my sorry-ass daddy to come out here and face me like a man!"

The door inched open enough for me to see her wide, frightened eyes. "He ain't here."

"You lying! Tell him to come to the door right now before I come in there and get his old a—"

"He ain't here. I don't know where he is. He left here hours ago. Said he was going fishing."

"If he ain't here, then why is his truck here?" I slurred.

"His truck *ain't* here."

I spun around and almost fell again. I peered into the darkness at the front yard—no truck and no boat. How had I missed that? Was I *that* drunk? "Damn, my bad," I said.

"Yeah," she replied before slamming the door shut.

I stumbled down the front steps and out into the yard to my car which was half in the yard and half in the road. I started the engine and fumbled with the gear shift before finally putting the car into reverse. I pulled onto the road and yawned and rubbed my eyes, and the next thing I knew, I was swerving across the center line, narrowly missing an oncoming car. I stopped in the middle of the road and shook my head. *Maybe I should just park this thing and walk home,* I thought. Before I could open the door to follow through on that thought—the only rational one I'd had that evening—the car I'd almost hit turned around and pulled up behind me. A big, tall man approached my car door and tapped on the window. "You almost hit me back there."

I nodded and offered him a sloppy smile. "I know. My bad. I think I'm gonna park this bad boy and walk home." I patted the steering wheel and reached for the door handle.

"Not so fast. You been drinking, son?"

I rolled my eyes. "Why? You think you the police or something?"

He pulled a badge out of his back pocket and flashed it at me. "As a matter of fact, I am."

I looked into the side view mirror, and for the first time, noticed that the car I'd almost hit was a police car. I focused on the man standing before me, noticed his uniform and hat. I studied his badge. Then I looked up at his face. "What's-what's your name, sir?" I asked.

"Deputy Donald Whimper."

"*Damn,*" I whispered.

***

I woke up the next afternoon, dazed and confused and in my own bed. Details of the previous night were pretty sketchy for me. I remembered Deputy Whimper arresting me. I remembered walking into the jail cell. I remembered worrying about my mother. But other than that, I had no recollection of how I got from the Lincoln County Jail in Star City back to my folks' house in Grady. But there I was, head throbbing, mouth stuck together, lying in my bed. The room smelled awful, or so I thought. It only took a few seconds for me to realize the smell was actually coming from me.

I sat up on the side of the bed and dropped my head. I was wearing the same clothes I'd worn the day before, and the smell was coming from them. My clothes smelled like a combination of cheap liquor, stale cigarettes, and puke. Since I didn't smoke, I was sure I'd picked up the cigarette smell in jail. I pulled my shirt over my head, blew my breath into my hand, and gagged. I shook my head, rubbed my hand across my hair, and stood from the bed. My bedroom door creaked open and a familiar face peeked inside.

"Hey, you're up. I was just peeking in here to check on you," Earl said in a gentle voice.

I smiled at my childhood friend. I should've known he'd come to my rescue. "Yeah, man. I'm okay. You bailed me out?"

He nodded as he stepped into the room. "Word gets around pretty quick here. As soon as I heard you'd been arrested, I bailed you out and brought you home. You were pretty wasted."

I hung my head slightly. I was forty-one years old—too old to be getting my first DUI. "Yeah. My damn life is—my life is kinda messed up, man. Got some messed up news yesterday. Guess I thought getting drunk would make me feel better."

He leaned against my dresser. "Did it?"

"What you think?"

"What happened, man?"

I hesitated. Earl was my friend, but what Latoya had told me was a bitter pill to swallow and the words tasted bad in my mouth. "Um... I talked to Latoya," I finally said.

Earl nodded. "And..."

"My daddy is her son's father."

Earl's eyes bulged and his mouth fell open. "What-how?"

"Evidently, they hooked up the summer after I left."

"Uh... Ivan... I don't know what to say."

I chuckled bitterly. "Yeah, I can understand that. Anyway, I left her place, paid a visit to WC, got drunk, and tried to kick my daddy's tail, but he wasn't home."

"WC still bootlegging?" he asked. "Ain't he about ninety years old now?"

"Yeah, he's still at it. Probably always be at it as long as this is a dry county. Seems like he's making that stuff stronger, too. I've never felt this bad after drinking."

"Well, I'm just glad you're okay."

I nodded, and my head began to spin. "I'm glad I didn't hurt anyone else. With the car, I mean. Driving drunk was a stupid move."

"I'd have to agree with that. Um, I brought your car back here for you, by the way."

"Thanks. Hey, is my mom okay?"

Earl smiled. "Yeah, she's good. Clear as a bell. She recognized me, asked about my folks."

"She ask about my dad?"

Earl shook his head. "No."

I scratched my head. "Funny thing is, she never even mentions him when her mind is clear, but he's all she talks about when the dementia is raging."

"I wonder why that is?"

"Man, I have no idea. Hey, thanks for bailing me out. I'm gonna pay you back as soon as I can. Right now, I'ma clean up and try to get my mind right. You don't have to stay."

He raised his eyebrows. "You sure?"

"Yeah."

"All right, but can you do me a favor, man?"

"Yeah, anything."

"Stay away from your dad until your mind is clear. I know you're upset with him, and you have every right to be, but I don't want to be preaching anyone's funeral over this."

"I ain't gon' fight him. It wouldn't really be a fair fight, anyway. It'd just be me punishing his old, geriatric tail. I'm done with him, though. He's as good as dead to me."

"He's your father."

"By DNA only. I hate him, Earl—for what he did to my mom all those years, and now? Leaving her like this? For taking advantage of Toya? I hate him."

"Like you said, he's an old man, and what happened with Toya was a long time ago, Ivan. I pray you forgive him before it's too late. You don't want to live with the guilt of not forgiving him if something happens to him."

"I'm good, man. I don't need to forgive him, and I don't think he cares who forgives him, anyway. I'm just glad I'm not like him."

Earl gave me a surprised look.

"Why you looking at me like that? You know I ain't nothing like him."

"Um, I should go. I'll check on you later, man. Take it easy."

"I will."

I watched him leave my bedroom, and then I headed to the bathroom to clean up.

21

"The News"

I heard you was looking for me, *boy*."

The voice came to me in the middle of the night, when I was fast asleep, and it scared the hell out of me. I sat straight up and rubbed my eyes. When the body standing over my bed finally came into focus, I felt my temper almost instantly rise to the point of explosion. I bolted to my feet and faced him with clenched fists. "Yeah, I been looking for you."

He stood there and stared at me. Then he smiled. "What you gon' do, boy? You gon' hit me?"

"I want to."

"Look, if you still upset about me leaving here, then I don't know what to tell you other than you need to get over it. I ain't coming back."

"Who the hell you think wants you around here?" I said through gritted teeth.

He looked a little surprised. "Then why you come over to my place scaring my woman like that?"

I banged my fist against the wall. "You screwed my girlfriend, Daddy."

He frowned slightly. "Which one? I done been with a lot of folks' girlfriends. Half of 'em I can't even remember they names."

I raised my fist. "You got this one pregnant."

He rubbed his chin and gave me a conceited grin. "Done that a bunch of times, too."

"Latoya Smith."

He shook his head slowly. "Hmm, name don't ring a bell. How old is the baby?"

"Twenty-two."

"Twenty-two? The hell you mad about this now for?"

"Because I love—I loved her. She was special to me."

He began to chuckle as he scratched his chin. "Yeah, well, I probably loved her for a second or two, myself. Still can't remember her, though. And I can't believe you mad at your own daddy about some woman. The hell wrong with you, boy? You wearing panties or boxers? I swear, you more sensitive than Imogene."

That was it. I lunged for him, knocking him into the dresser and sending everything on it crashing to the floor. One thing I figured out quickly: the old man still had some strength in him. He pushed against me and we tussled for a good while before the CNA came into the room, screaming.

"Something is wrong with Ms. Versie!" she shrieked.

I released the strangle-hold I had on my father and followed the aide to my mother's room. My father staggered down the hall and out the front door without even peeping in on my mother. When I saw my mother, she looked fine. "What's going on?" I asked as I turned to face the aide.

"I'm sorry, Mr. Ivan. I lied. Your mama heard all of the commotion, and she asked me to do something to stop y'all. She was so upset. I was just trying to help."

I blew out a breath. "Yeah, well, you probably kept me from murdering him. So, thank you… I guess."

"Sweetheart, can you leave me and my son alone?" Mama said.

"Yes, ma'am."

After the aide left, Mama reached for my hand. "Sit down, Ivan."

I was glad her mind was clear at the moment, but deep inside, I still wanted to follow Daddy and run his truck off the road. Instead, I sat down in a chair next to her bed and gripped her hand in mine. "Yes, Mama?"

"What was going on earlier… with you and your daddy?" she asked.

"Nothing… we just had words. You know we haven't ever really gotten along."

She sighed. "You found out about that girl you used to like and her baby, didn't you?"

I frowned as I looked her in the eye. "Yes, ma'am."

"And you're angry?"

"Yes, ma'am. I… I hate him for doing that to her. I cared about her, and she didn't deserve to have to raise a child alone. Life's been hard for her, Mama. *I hate him.*"

"Then you may as well hate me, too."

I shook my head. *Damn, her mind is going again.* "What are you talking about, Mama?"

"If you hate your daddy, then you gotta hate me, too. I knew about that girl and her baby, and I didn't do nothing to help her, either. I didn't do nothing to help none of them. I just… I just sat back and let it happen."

I shook my head again. "None of them? How… how many are there, Mama? I mean, I always knew about his outside kids, but how many exactly?"

She sighed. "I don't have no idea, baby. A lot, that's for sure. It don't really matter. What matters is that I knew, and I just sat up in here and let it happen. I should've made your daddy be more responsible. But…"

"What, Mama? But, what?"

"But I didn't do a thing."

I dropped my head then looked back up at Mama. "Mama, can I ask you something?"

She nodded. "You wanna know why I never left him, don't you?"

"Yes, ma'am. I don't understand it."

She reached over and placed her free hand on top of our joined ones. "Well, at first it was because I was crazy about him. Your daddy was a handsome man—still is. You just like him, baby. Handsome as all get out."

I smiled.

"And he was older than me, had a good job, too. When we started courting, I was the envy of every girl in the county. Everybody wanted to be gray-eyed Wardell Spencer's girl, and nobody could believe he picked *me*—chubby, short, little Versie Lowe. But he did. And for a long time, I think I held on to him just to spite everyone who said it wouldn't work out. It was hard, and I cried many a night because of the rumors that turned out to be true, and the women…

the women who would come knocking at my door with their babies on their hips and tears in their eyes, because my husband had broken their hearts.

"And then he gave me you… and then Imogene. And I knew I could never leave him. I was so thankful for my babies, my pretty babies. Wardell makes the prettiest babies, you know? And he was a good provider. And he never raised his hand to me. I can't say that much for a lot of the husbands of the women I've known. So many of them were getting knocked around. But your daddy was never violent towards me or you kids, and we never wanted for nothing. I felt like that was worth staying for. I didn't have no education, baby. Wasn't no way I could provide for you and your sister.

"And after you kids was grown, it didn't make no sense to leave him after all those years. So I stayed." She looked toward the ceiling. "And I'm still here. And he gone."

I frowned and wondered just how much of what was going on Mama was aware of. She was in and out of being in her right mind so much, it was hard to tell. "You know where he's staying now, Mama?" I asked.

She looked over at me. "Mm-hmm. I imagine he over there with Ebony Goodloe and them kids she done had by him and whoever else."

I stared at her for a moment. "You know about her?"

"I know about all of them, Ivan. Your daddy ain't never tried to keep his cheating a secret. Everybody know. Everybody always knew. I used to hear them whispering at church about poor Versie and that lowdown Wardell, but half of them was sleeping with him, too."

"I don't understand why everybody still wants him."

She chuckled lightly. "You'd have to be a woman to understand that, baby. It's probably the same reason women like you. They do like you, don't they?"

I dropped my eyes and felt a little strange about this part of the conversation. "Um, yes, ma'am. They do."

"You treating them right?"

I nodded. "Yes, ma'am. I don't lie to them. They know where they stand."

"Hmm, we women are funny. We love hard, and sometimes we go along with things we don't agree with and say we understand when we really don't."

"Why?"

"Because that's how a lot of us love. Through sacrifice. Sometimes, we willing to sacrifice a little happiness just to be with the man we love. Sometimes, we sacrifice facing the truth, too. And a lot of times, we end up getting hurt. Be careful who you hurt, baby, even if you're not trying to hurt them. The Bible can't lie. You reap what you sow."

"Yes, ma'am. I hear you."

She yawned. "I hope you do. Listen baby, forgive your daddy, and let him live his life. He gon' reap his, too. You can best believe that. He got his to reap, and I got mine. We all do."

I nodded, stood from the chair, leaned over, and kissed her on the forehead. "Get some rest, Mama. I love you."

She reached up and placed each of her hands on the sides of my face. "I love you too, baby. I don't ever want you to forget that."

"I won't, Mama."

I hated to leave her, because I was afraid this was the last time her mind would be clear. I was always afraid of that, afraid that her mind would completely slip away because of this horrible disease. But she was tired, and so was I. So I could only pray that her mind would be clear in the morning and that maybe, just maybe, we could continue our conversation.

***

Mama was confused again the next morning. The daytime aide called in sick, but the agency sent a replacement. After getting her acclimated to Mama's routine, I showered, dressed, and told her I was heading out for some fresh air. I had a lot on my mind—what Mama said about forgiving Daddy and her role in the things he did. No matter what she said, I couldn't place the blame on her. Daddy was a grown man who'd scattered kids all over the place and didn't bother to even really own them, let alone take care of them. He was a despicable man who skated through life on the power of his penis. He was as good as dead to me.

I walked over to my car, unlocked the door, and then locked it again, deciding to take a walk instead. I left my parents' property and turned onto the road toward a destination unknown. I walked for a good while, turning right and then left and then right again. I was sweating up my jeans and t-shirt by the time I reached her house. And as I stood at her front door with my fist raised in preparation of knocking, I had no idea why I was there. I guess I just needed to see her.

The door creaked open to reveal Latoya standing there in another barely there pair of shorts and a baggy t-shirt. With curiosity in her pretty eyes, she said, "Ivan?"

"Yeah, uh… good morning, Toya. Can I… can I come in?"

She hesitated, nodded, and let me in. She offered me a seat and a beverage. "No, I'm not thirsty," I lied as I took a seat on her sofa. I felt like it would be wrong to drink her water. Anything I took from her would be wrong.

"You sure? You sweating."

I rubbed my sweaty hands across the thighs of my jeans and looked down at my shirt. "Yeah, I guess a cup of water would be good."

She left, swinging her hips all the way to her kitchen. When she made it back, I looked up at her, took the cool cup of water from her hand, and smiled. "Thanks." I gulped it down in seconds.

"What's up, Ivan?"

"Um… where's Charles?"

She shrugged. "I'm not sure. He didn't come home last night."

I frowned. "Really?"

"Yeah, he does that sometimes. He's grown, so I don't really worry about it. But I do wish he'd hang around here more and help me." She rested her head on the back of the easy chair she was sitting in and closed her eyes. "Lord knows I need some help."

"Help with what?"

She opened her eyes and looked at me. "Nothing for you to worry about. Just life. Just *my* life. It is what it's always been… a struggle."

"A financial struggle? I could help." That wasn't really true. My bank account was bleeding, and I was steadily losing money, but I felt like I needed to say it. It was the least I could do to try and offer her some comfort in some form.

"Financial, emotional, you name it. I'm just… I'm just tired, and last night was a bad night for us."

"For who?"

She stared at me for a moment. "Never mind. Why am I telling you all of this anyway? You don't care, and I know you didn't come over here to listen to my problems. Charles is not here right now, so is that all you wanted? To talk to him?"

"No… I wanted to see you. To tell you that I know what happened with my father wasn't your fault. And for the record, I do care about your problems." I leaned forward and rested my elbows on my knees. "I care about you, Toya. And I'm sorry for leaving you hanging like that back in the day. I want to be here for you now."

She sighed. "Ivan—"

An alarm sounded loudly, cutting her off. It was different from the one I'd heard the other day. Her eyes dashed toward the hallway, and a second later, she was on her feet. I stood and followed her down the hallway to a room, and my eyes widened. Lying in a bed was a young girl hooked up to all kinds of machines. The girl was beautiful, just like Latoya. Was this her daughter?

As Latoya frantically pushed buttons on a machine and tinkered with a tube that ran from the machine into the girl's mouth, I just stood there—frozen. Latoya was whispering, "Come on, come on, breathe, baby. Breathe."

I snapped out of my stupor, reached into my pocket, pulled out my cell phone, and dialed 911.

The paramedics had a hard time getting her to breathe again, but, thankfully, they did. Latoya rode with her daughter in the ambulance, and I ran back to my house to get my car. I raced to the hospital in Pine Bluff to see what was going on. I knew Latoya must've been on pins and needles. I wanted to be there for her.

I also wanted to understand. Whenever she had mentioned her daughter in the past, she never mentioned her condition. Not once. I wondered what had happened to her. Was she born sick? Was that who Latoya was visiting in the hospital that time? What was going on?

I met her in the ER waiting area where she sat with her head in her hands. I sat down beside her and softly patted her back. She looked up at me with tears streaming down her face. "Ivan..." She collapsed against me, and I pulled her close.

"Hey, I'm here. I'm not going anywhere," I said softly as I rubbed my hand up and down her arm. "I'm not going anywhere, Toya."

We sat there for a long time, her crying, me trying to comfort her and block out the questions that kept running through my mind. I knew that more than anything, she just needed someone to be there. I felt that comfort was something Latoya had been without for a long time.

"Do you feel like telling me what's going on, Toya? I mean, if you don't, you don't have to."

She looked up at me, took a deep breath, and wiped her eyes. "She was, um... she was always such a sweet girl and so smart, you know? Her daddy left when she was little and never looked back, but she was an angel, Ivan. Such a good girl, no trouble at all."

I smiled at her.

"I, uh, lost my job when she was eight. Recession and all, you know?"

I nodded.

"And, um… we had to move into an apartment in a bad part of town. Drugs, gangs, you name it. I hated it, but it was all I could afford. I didn't have any help. No child support. Hell, I didn't even know where her father was so I *could* file on him. And well, by that time, Charles was eighteen, and I didn't see the point in filing on your daddy."

I nodded slightly. Just hearing her mention my father made me want to climb in my car and mow him down on some deserted road. I seriously wanted to punch his lights out.

"One night, we heard some shots, but that wasn't anything we weren't used to. Usually, you'd here a couple of shots and that would be that. But this time, whoever it was kept shooting. And the sound kept getting closer. Charles wasn't home, and I started to get a little scared. I hoped he wasn't somewhere in the middle of some gang shootout. He was a good boy, but he grew up without a father, and he had some anger issues, still does.

"I'd grabbed my phone and was dialing 911 when the bullets shattered the glass in my living room window. I hit the floor, told my baby, Asia, to do the same. But… but it was too late. It was too late…"

Tears began to fill her eyes again. "She was shot twice in the back. You don't know what it's like to have to hold your child, your baby, in your arms and think they're going to die. She was so little and there was so much blood, and I thought I lost her that night. But, thank God, I didn't. She made it. It was a struggle, Ivan. But she made it.

"Her spinal cord was damaged, and she's paralyzed. She has trouble breathing on her own. She has to wear diapers. But she's still sweet and funny and smart. She's still my Asia. I just wish…"

I reached for her hand and squeezed it in mine. "What, Toya?"

"I can't take care of her like I need to. I... I have to do everything, Ivan. *Everything*. She's on Medicaid, and they won't pay for a nurse to come in and help me anymore. I don't even know why. I'm appealing, but in the meantime, I have to do everything for her, and... and I'm so tired. But she's my baby, and I'm not putting her in no home. Charles helps sometimes, but she's not his responsibility, and I can't expect him to just sit around the house all the time. I'm trying, but she keeps getting bladder infections from the catheter, or lung infections, or bed sores. She's in and out of the hospital so much, there's no way I can keep a job and pay someone to come in and help." She pulled away from me and covered her face with her hands.

"She was in the hospital the last time my mama was, wasn't she? That's who you were here to see?"

She nodded, looked up at me with weary eyes. "Ivan, I'm just so tired... I feel like I'm failing her."

"Ms. Smith, we've got her stabilized now. You can come back and see her," a nurse who seemed to appear out of nowhere said.

Latoya looked at me, relief on her face. Then she stood and followed the nurse through the doors that led into the ER unit. I settled in my seat and sighed. I was feeling something I'd never felt before. My heart actually ached for Latoya. Everything in me wanted to make things right for her, but I had no idea what to do other than be there for her. I leaned forward, rested my elbows on my knees, and stared at my reflection on the shiny linoleum floor.

"What you doing here?"

I looked up to see Charles standing over me. I sat up straight. "I'm here with your mother."

He sat across from me and glanced around the waiting area. "Where is she? She texted me and said she was bringing my little sister to the hospital."

I nodded. "She's back there with her. Your sister gave us quite a scare, but the nurse said she's stable now."

He frowned slightly. "Gave *us* a scare? Who the hell is *us*? What you got to do with my sister, man?"

I held up my hands. "Look, Charles, I'm just here to support your mom. That's it. I'm not here to start anything with you."

He scoffed. "Support her? Really? My mama done struggled my whole damn life, and you wanna support her *now*? Where the hell were you and your family when I was walking around with holes in my shoes? You were supposed to be some kind of whack rapper back then, right? Couldn't spare some change for your little brother? Man, you and your *support* can go straight to hell."

"I didn't know about you, Charles. If I had, I would've helped. If you wanna be mad, be mad at our father. He's to blame for this… for *all* of this."

"You think I ain't mad at him?!" he asked, raising his voice. "I *hate* him."

I leaned back in my chair. "Yeah, well, join the club."

His frown diminished, and he leaned back a little. "Oh, yeah. What he do to you?"

I looked him in the eye. "He hurt your mama. I loved her."

He shook his head. "You and every other dude that broke her heart."

I couldn't think of anything to say in response, because he was right, and I knew it. I *had* broken her heart. A part of me felt responsible for how her life had turned out. If only I hadn't left her behind and never looked back—

My cell phone rang, interrupting my thoughts. I stood from my seat and rushed outside when I saw the call was coming from my parents' house. "Hello?"

"Mr. Spencer?"

"Yes?"

"This is Simona, the substitute aide?"

"Yes."

"I'm sorry to bother you, but your mother is really agitated, and I don't know what to do to calm her down."

"Can you put her on the phone?"

"Sure."

A second later, I heard my mother's voice, screaming something I couldn't understand. "Mama!" I shouted. "Mama, it's Ivan. Mama, what's going on? What's wrong?"

"Wardell? Wardell, where you at?! Where the hell you at?!" She was crying. She sounded almost hysterical.

"Mama, it's Ivan. It's your son, Mama."

"Wardell, I ain't got time to play with you. I need to know if you gon' keep your promise. You not gonna tell, are you? You promised not to tell!"

"Mama… Mama, listen. This is your son, Ivan. Not Wardell. Not my daddy. It's Ivan. I want you to try to calm down."

"Please don't tell him. Please, Wardell. Please don't tell Ivan I'm not his mother. You promised. You promised..."

22

"Matter of Time"

I don't know how I held it together long enough to walk back inside that waiting room and wait for Latoya to return. I needed to leave, to figure out what my mother was talking about, but I didn't want to leave without telling Latoya goodbye and hearing what she had to say about her daughter's condition.

I had managed to calm Mama down by pretending to be my father and promising not to tell myself that she wasn't my mother. But I was sure she didn't know what she was talking about. Of course she was my mother... wasn't she? She had to be. If not, that would mean my whole life had been a lie. *My whole life.*

I sat there, staring at the floor, waiting for Latoya. Charles didn't say a word to me after I walked back into the waiting room. I figured it was because my demeanor had changed. When something worries me, I get this look on my face that tells people not to bother me. I was sure I was wearing that look as I tried to make sense of what my mother had just said. *It was the dementia talking*, I told myself. And then myself told me, *she rants and raves when she's confused, but she never lies. She never lies.*

I leaned back in my chair and blew out a frustrated breath. Charles looked up at me and said, "Uh, you all right, man? You really worried about my sister, huh?"

I nodded. "Yeah, her and a lot of other things."

He tapped his foot a few times and then leaned forward. "Hey, um… what's my daddy like?"

With raised eyebrows, I said, "He's…" I sighed. "Look, you didn't miss nothing. I promise you didn't."

He nodded. "Did he hit you and stuff? Was he mean?"

I shook my head. "He's not violent. He never was. He was just… absent. My daddy lived in the house with me, and I barely saw him. He stayed out in the streets more than anything, He paid the bills and gave me his last name. That's about the extent of our relationship, and right now, he's really a non-factor in my life."

He raised his eyebrows. "Oh."

"Sorry if that wasn't what you wanted to hear."

"Naw, it's all good. I mean, I know he sorry, got to be to leave my mama hanging like that. I just wonder about him sometimes. Like, how he looks. I ain't never seen him."

I shrugged. "Looking at me and you is as good as looking at him. We both look just like him. Tall, brown skin, gray eyes." I gave him a slight smile. "Handsome."

He smiled a little, too. "Yeah, I figured that since we look so much alike and we ain't even got the same mama."

I nodded and thought to myself that Charles was the lucky one of us two. He'd never had Wardell Spencer in his life, and he knew who his mother was. As of a few minutes earlier, I didn't have a clue who mine was. That thought made my head tighten. I was ready to leave and get to the bottom of this. I was ready for someone to explain what my mother had said.

I'd almost decided to leave without saying goodbye to Latoya when she finally returned. Charles stood and hugged her. I stood by and watched.

"How she doing, Mama?" Charles asked.

She gave him a small smile. I could tell she was trying to be brave. "She's got a bad lung infection, but she's better. They're getting ready to move her to ICU."

"She gon' be all right?" he asked.

She reached up and rubbed his cheek. "I hope so." She turned to me. "You waited? You didn't have to do that."

I shoved my hands into the pockets of my jeans. "I wanted to be sure she was okay. Um… I do need to go, though. I need to check on my mom. The aide called a few minutes ago and my mom was really agitated."

She nodded. "Yes, go. Go check on your mother. I totally understand. I'm gonna spend the night here."

"Okay, can I call you later?" I asked.

"Sure. If you want to."

I leaned in and kissed her cheek, then I nodded at Charles and left.

***

This was getting to be a habit—me standing at this door, beating on it, watching it shake on its hinges, inspecting the torn screen while I waited. She opened it after only about thirty seconds of my persistent knocking. She was wearing a frown and a short dress. When she saw that it was me, she turned and called his name without really acknowledging me.

"Wardell! It's for you!" she said, and then she disappeared back into the trailer, the inside of which I was sure matched the outside—cluttered and unclean.

A minute or so later, I heard my father's shuffling feet as he walked to the door. He peered at me, smacked his lips, and rubbed his stomach. "Caught me in the middle of dinner, boy. What you here for? Wanna fight me, again?"

"Who is my mother?"

His face dropped and he leaned against the door facing. He stared at the floor for a long while. "Who told you?"

I gasped and backed away a little. It was true? Versie Spencer, the only woman I'd ever called "Mama" was not my mother? "M… Mama did. She thought I was you. She begged me/you not to tell me that she wasn't my mother."

He shook his head. "All these years, she was worried about me telling, and she the one that told. I knew she was gon' tell it one day after her mind starting going."

I stared at him, willing myself not to knock him into the next week. "You didn't answer my question. Who is my mother? My *real* mother?"

"Versie your real mama."

"You basically just admitted that the woman who raised me is not my mother, so who is?"

"Now, listen. She let the cat out the bag, but I ain't gon' set him free. Maybe she'll tell you one day, but I ain't tellin'. I promised her a long time ago—"

Before I realized what I was doing, I had grabbed my father by his collar and lifted him off of his feet. "I'm not playing with you, old man! You ain't never kept a promise in your whole damn life! I got a right to know who my mother is, and you are gonna tell me!"

His eyes were wide as he said, "Erma… Erma is your mother."

23

"Why"

I sat in my car in my aunt's driveway, staring at her front porch and trying to decide if I really wanted to face her. Her house was neat, had always been. Her yard was always neatly trimmed and so were her rose bushes. I hadn't been inside her house in years, but I was sure the inside was just as neat as it always had been. I could remember visiting her as a boy, how clean everything always was— neat with nothing out of place. She was always so nice to me, called me her favorite nephew. Treated me like the son she never had.

The son she never had.

She had a daughter, Gracie. Me and Gracie were never really close, but she was really close to Imogene when we were growing up. Cousin Gracie. My sister, Gracie? Was Imogene still my sister? Who was her mother?

I shook my head and then rested it against the headrest. I closed my eyes and took a deep breath as I tried to pull myself together. I was angry, too angry to talk to anyone at that moment. Shoot, the only reason I didn't throttle my father was because of the shock of hearing that my aunt was really my mother. After that, I'd let him go and stumbled to my car. That was all I *could* do. And now I sat in her driveway, wanting to hear it from her mouth and not wanting to hear it, too.

My aunt is really my mother.

My mother is really my aunt.

Then other thoughts, words, invaded my mind:

"Baby, I don't know a woman in this county with a working vagina that ain't slept with your daddy."

"Wardell makes the prettiest babies, you know?"

Then I thought about how happy Aunt Erma always was to see me, how tightly she'd hug me. All the things she'd said about my father. How she despised him. What was going on? How could *she* be my mother?

My eyes popped open at the sound of someone tapping on my window. Aunt Erma was standing next to the car with a concerned look on her face. "Ivan? You okay in there?" she asked through the glass.

I stared at her for a moment, fully realizing for the first time, that this short little woman, a woman I'd always known as my favorite aunt, was actually my mother.

My mother.

She backed away from the car as I opened the door and stepped onto the ground. Gravel crunched under my feet as I stood beside her, looking down at her. At first, she wore a look of confusion, and then, I think she realized I knew, that her forty-one-year-old secret had been revealed. She dropped her eyes and pulled the belt of her robe tighter around her waist. She didn't say a word for several minutes, and neither did I. We just stood there, me staring at her, her eyes glued to the ground. We just stood there as dusk settled around us.

A car passed by on the road, startling both of us as the driver honked his or her horn. She finally lifted her eyes and looked past me toward the road. "That was Ivory Wilkerson. You remember him, don't you? I think he has a son around your age. You probably went to school with him."

I glanced at the road and then back at her. I shook my head.

She looked up at me with a strained expression. "You wanna come inside?"

I nodded and followed her into her immaculate house. I sat at her kitchen table and watched as she fixed both of us glasses of her famous peach lemonade. She set the tall glass in front of me and then settled in the chair across from me. She wrapped a bony hand around her glass of lemonade, and with her eyes settled on the table, she said, "I knew Versie was gonna be the one to tell it. As soon as we found out she had the Alzheimer's, I knew she was gon' eventually tell it. You finding out the truth was her worst fear. She worried about it all the time, studied on it, you know? She studied on it just like she did the way your daddy treated her. And she was so scared he was gonna leave her, begged him to stay more times than I wanna remember. You spend all your time thinking about something, and it's bound to come out in the wash eventually. It's bound to happen."

I pushed my glass aside and rested my hands on the table. "Why?"

She looked up at me with sorrow and regret in her eyes. "Why, what? Why'd I sleep with Wardell? Why'd I give you to Versie?"

I nodded. "That's a start."

"The first thing you need to know is how much I love you, Ivan. I love you more than anything in this whole world."

I raised an eyebrow and scoffed.

"It's the truth. I love Gracie, but you're my first born. There's a special place in my heart for you. Always has been and always will be."

145

I leaned back in my chair and folded my arms over my chest.

She shifted her eyes back to the table. "I was young, so young when your ma—when Versie married Wardell. She wasn't but eighteen herself. And I was sixteen. We were close, and I missed her after she moved out, so she would let me spend the night with them sometimes. She said she got lonely, because Wardell would be gone so much. He started cheating on my sister before the ink was dry on their marriage license, was gone all the time. So it was fun for us to spend time together. Plus, after she left home, I became the oldest, and I got tired of watching our little brothers and cooking and cleaning. Staying over at Versie's place was like a vacation to me."

She sighed. "When I turned eighteen, I moved in with Versie and Wardell for good. Got me a little job cleaning up for a couple of the white ladies across the tracks. Wardell would take me to work and pick me up. And… and before long, he started giving me these looks and rubbing on my thighs when we would be in his car." She looked up at me again. "I'm not going to sit here and put all the blame on him, though. Truth is, I liked Wardell, thought he was handsome. And I didn't have no boyfriend… and I envied Versie, I really did. As low down as Wardell was and still is, he was a catch. Wasn't a girl around for miles that didn't want to be in Versie's shoes. Not a one.

"I felt real bad after we were together that first time. Couldn't even look my sweet sister in the eye for a week. But after that, it got easier. That's how it is with sin, you know? The more you practice it, the easier it gets. Anyhow, the next thing I knew, I was in love with him, or at least I thought I was. When I found out I was pregnant and told him, all of that changed. He was… he was so mean to me. Told me it was my problem, that he wasn't leaving Versie, and that he didn't care about me. I was so hurt, Ivan. I was so hurt. I packed my stuff and ran back home and told my mama.

"She told me I deserved to be hurt for doing that to my own sister, and you know what? She was right. Hurt was all I deserved for doing that to my sweet, sweet sister. My mama told me to go back and tell Versie what I did and ask her for forgiveness." She stopped and stood from the table. She walked over to the kitchen counter and grabbed some paper towels. Then she reclaimed her seat at the table.

She wiped her wet face and continued: "I was so afraid to tell Versie, because I knew it would break her heart. But I did what my mother told me to do. I went to her and told her and asked her to forgive me. The first thing she said was that she wanted the baby. That the only way she would forgive me was if I gave her the baby. Then she went on and on about how Wardell had gotten babies all over the county and that meant she must not have been able to have babies. She said my baby would be the closest thing to being hers."

"So you gave me to her?"

She nodded. "Wasn't no way for me to take care of you on my own, Ivan. And I wanted to make my sister happy."

"So you just handed me over like I was a damn toy?"

She shook her head. "No! I can't tell you how hard it was for me to give you to her. How hard it was to watch you grow up right in front of me, to hear you call me auntie. It was the hardest thing I've ever done in my life."

"Why did y'all have to lie about it? I'm forty-one! Y'all were gonna take this to the grave, weren't you?"

She dabbed her eyes with the paper towel. "Versie didn't want you to know the truth. She wanted you to believe she was your mother. Who were me and Wardell to argue with her?"

I nodded. "Imogene yours, too?"

"No. Versie is her mama. She was a surprise. I guess Versie was just real hard to get pregnant."

I rested my elbows on the table and rubbed my hands over my hair.

"Please don't hate me," she said softly. "It was a hard thing for me to do, but it was the right thing. Versie was a good mother to you, better than I ever could've been."

I didn't lift my head or say a word in response.

"I hope that one day you will forgive me," she said.

I looked up at her for a moment, then I stood from the table, and left.

***

I stopped by the bootlegger's on the way home and got me a pint of gin. At home, I bypassed my mother's room, headed to mine, and shut the door behind me. I fell into my bed and closed my eyes, clutching the unopened bottled of gin to my chest. This time, I was going to get drunk in the confines of my room. No more DUIs.

I sat up, unscrewed the cap, took a swig, and let out a grunt. Then I took another swig as I tried to erase the pitiful look my aunt/mother wore on her face when she told me about her affair with my father from my mind. I tried to block out her rationality that giving me to her sister had been the "right" thing. I tried to forget the lifetime of lies I'd been told. I tried not to hate my father any more at that moment than I had before. And I tried not to be angry at the woman who raised me, the woman I had known and loved as my mother my entire life. But she was a liar, too, wasn't she? She was a liar, too.

I emptied that bottle and in no time, felt a nice buzz. Some of my emotions were numb. I wasn't as angry, but I was sad. I was keenly aware of a sense of sorrow that seemed to fill me from head to toe. I think I was sad about the fact that the one mainstay in my life wasn't real. My mother, who'd always loved and cared for me, who'd always been an angel in my eyes, wasn't really my mother at all. I suddenly felt like I really didn't know who I was anymore. Everyone had let me down. *Everyone*.

As I drifted off to sleep, I thought about Latoya and how she probably felt like everyone had let her down, too. I wanted to call to check on her, but my eyes were too heavy. And so was my heart.

24

"Hard to Breathe"

I woke up the next morning with a pounding headache, to the sound of someone knocking at my bedroom door. I stumbled out of bed and answered it to find the night aide standing on the other side wearing a worried look on her face. I stood a little taller and tried to appear normal although I was sure I looked pretty hung over standing there wearing the same clothes from the day before.

"Yes?" I said.

"Um, Mr. Spencer, the day shift aide is running late, but she's on her way, and I gotta get on home and put my kids on the school bus. Can you sit with your mother until the other girl gets here? I've already washed her up. She's sitting at the kitchen table in her wheelchair. Maybe you can give her a little breakfast?"

I nodded as I rubbed my head. "Yeah, go ahead. Thanks for letting me know what's going on."

She smiled, gave me a little nod, and ducked out of my room. I headed to the bathroom, saw my red eyes in the mirror, and shook my head as I splashed water on my face. My stomach was bubbling, and my headache was getting worse by the second. And the crazy thing was, I was ready for another trip to the bootlegger's. There was no way I was going to be able to stay in that town, *in that house*, sober.

I dried my hands on my t-shirt and shuffled up the hall to the kitchen where my mother sat staring into space. I could tell her mind was somewhere else, and I was glad. I don't think I would've been able to deal with her if she'd been at herself.

"You hungry, Mama?" For the first time in my life, calling her that felt wrong. But what else was I supposed to call her?

She looked up at me and smiled. "Ivan? That you? Boy, when you get here?"

I sighed softly. Maybe it would've been better if she *was* aware of herself. I was almost too tired and hung over to spend the day explaining everything to her over and over again. "I been here for weeks. Don't you remember?" I tried not to sound irritated, but it was hard. Her accidental revelation had robbed me of what was left of my patience.

"You have? Sho' nuff? Naw, I don't remember, baby. But I'm glad you here. I missed you."

I sat down across from her, looked into her eyes, and saw the genuine love that had always been there. "Yeah, I'm glad I'm here, too."

"Where's your daddy? I'm hungry? We got any ribs?"

"He's not here, Mama. It's breakfast time. Want me to fix you some eggs?"

She shook her head. "Come sit next to me. I'm so glad you're here! I missed you."

I hung my head a little. She was killing me. I left my chair and sat in the one right next to her. She smiled and reached for me, to hug me. She pulled me close to her, and I laid my head on her shoulder. She rubbed her hand over my hair and said, "My baby. I'm so glad my baby is here."

I closed my eyes and felt them well up. It was too much—

knowing the truth was too much. I loved my mama too much for her not to be my mama. I hated my father. I didn't know how I felt about Erma. I was worried about Latoya and her daughter and what would become of them. I felt bad for Charles. It was all too much. It was suffocating me.

I couldn't stay there any longer. It was too hard. I was too angry at everyone, and it was eating me alive.

I shed a few tears there on my mother's shoulder, and she comforted me, told me everything was going to be okay. I wished she knew what she was talking about. I wished there was some way the truth could disappear and I could go back to the life I once knew.

***

"Where is he?" I asked as I stared at the young woman through her raggedy screen door.

"Fishing," she said, her eyes glued to me.

"Where?"

She shrugged slightly. "Vlen Lake, I think."

I turned to leave, but her voice stopped me. "Hey, you thirsty or anything?"

I frowned as I turned around to face her. "What?"

She dropped her eyes coyly. "I was wondering if you was thirsty. You can come in and have a drink. I got water and Kool-Aid and milk. It's all cold." She fluttered her eyelashes. I chuckled softly as I realized she was flirting with me.

"Nah, I'm good," I replied. Then I turned to leave again.

"Humph, I bet you are," she said softly.

I turned back around. "What the hell is wrong with you? You shacked up with my married father who you claim you got some kids by, and you up here flirting with me. You must be out your mind if you think I'd touch you."

She smirked. "I heard you was with Donna Whimper. I know I look better than her, so I figured I'd give it a shot. You gon' stand there and tell me you don't want me?"

I stepped a little closer to her and said, "Not no, but *hell*, no."

She rolled her neck and said, "So, what? You too good for me?"

I nodded. "Considering the fact that you're laying up in here with my daddy when my mother, his *wife*, is wasting away, I'd say yeah, I'm *way* too good for you."

I eyed her for a second, and then I left.

I headed over to the lake where I found my father sitting on the bank holding an extra-long, cane pole. He looked like he was at peace out there on the lake, and that only served to piss me off more. If I couldn't have peace, he didn't deserve to have it, either.

"Daddy," I said as I stepped up behind him.

He jumped and almost dropped the pole. "Boy, you scared the hell outta me! You can't just sneak up on a man like that. You lucky I ain't got my gun with me."

"Yeah, whatever. Look, I need you to get in your truck and follow me."

"Follow you where?"

"You'll see when we get there."

"Now, look. I ain't going—"

"No, *you* look. I'm telling you to get in that truck and follow me right now. I'm not playing with you, Daddy. I'm done playing games with you. Get in that damn truck, *now*!"

He looked startled, and after sitting there for a minute or two, he stood to his feet with a grunt and walked over to his truck, set his fishing pole in the bed, and climbed into the cab. "Don't drive too fast. I need some tires, and I don't wanna get a blowout on these bad roads out here," he said.

I nodded, climbed into my car, and pulled onto the road.

About fifteen minutes later, we were pulling into Erma's driveway. I was relieved to see her dusty red Buick sitting in her yard. I climbed out of the car and watched Daddy slide out of his truck with a confused look on his face. "What's going on?" he asked. "What we doing at Erma's?"

"You'll see when we get inside."

"She probably ain't gon' let me in there."

"She will today. For me."

I led him to the door where I knocked and shouted, "It's Ivan!" before she could say, "Who is it?"

The door creaked open a minute later to reveal the tiny woman, who'd always been short and thin and pretty—much prettier than the woman who raised me. She was wearing a long yellow caftan with a matching turban on her head. She gave me a small smile and then, noticing my father behind me, let the smile fade away. "What's going on?" she asked.

"We need to talk. *All of us*. Can we come in?" I said.

"*You* can come in. Not *him*," was her response.

"The only way I'm coming in is with him."

She stood there for a few seconds and then opened the door wide enough for me and Daddy to pass through. We sat in her living room this time, silent at first. Then Daddy spoke.

"Why we here, Ivan? You know the truth. What else you need to hear?"

"I need for the two of you to step up and help Mama. You owe her. You both do. I can't do it anymore. I'm angry at her, at all of y'all. But mostly at her, and I can't stand feeling that way about her. I can't be here anymore, but I'm not putting her in a nursing home. She doesn't deserve that. Not since she's the only somebody who ever cared about me."

"I care about you, Ivan," Erma said.

I snapped my head in her direction. "You do? Coulda fooled me since you handed me off like a damn piece of paper."

I could see tears forming in her eyes, but I didn't care. She bit her bottom lip and looked away.

"And you said you couldn't stand to sit with her anymore because she was lashing out at you. From where I sit, you deserve everything she throws at you, *Aunt* Erma," I added.

"You tryna punish us or something?" Daddy asked. "I done already told you that I moved on. I got me another family to—"

I raised my hand and shook my head. "I ain't tryna hear that today, Daddy. That trick you shacked up with just tried to get with me. My mama has never disrespected you like that, even though you have done nothing but disrespect her. You owe her, man. You owe her more than anyone in the world. She's… she's disappearing, and she needs you there. You need to be there for her."

I stood from the sofa. "Y'all need to figure something out. Y'all can take turns staying with her. One of y'all can move in. I don't care. But I can't be there anymore. I need to get back to my own life, and I need to do it *today*." I walked to the door.

"Where you going? I'm parked behind you," Daddy called after me.

"I can get around your truck."

I left, slamming the door behind me.

I'd only been back at the house for an hour or so when I heard the knock at the front door. I didn't move a muscle, figuring that the aide would get it, and she did. A minute later, there was a knock at my open bedroom door, and I turned to see Erma there, still wearing that gold caftan and turban and holding a small suitcase. I stared at her, more than surprised to see her.

Her eyes were on the floor as she said, "I'ma stay here with Versie. You can leave whenever you're ready."

"Thank you," I said.

She nodded and as she turned to leave, said, "I'm sorry, Ivan. I'm sorry about everything."

I didn't reply, but watched her disappear from my doorway.

I packed my stuff up in record time, stopped by my sleeping mother's room and kissed her goodbye, then left my childhood home.

25

"Everybody Knows"

At the airport, I bought a ticket to Atlanta and waited at my gate for the flight, which departed in four hours. While sitting there, I dialed Latoya's cell phone number and smiled when I heard her soft, "Hello?"

"Hey, Toya. It's Ivan. You all right? How's your little girl?"

"I'm fine, and Asia is a lot better. She might get to go home next week, and the social worker is gonna set up some home health for her."

"Good. I'm glad to hear that. Hey, I wanted to let you know that I'm heading back to Atlanta in a couple of hours."

"Really?" She sounded a little disappointed. "Well, I'll... you have a safe trip, Ivan. Okay?"

"I'll try."

"When will you be back?"

"I don't know, Toya. Probably not for a long time. I can't... I don't wanna be there anymore."

"Oh."

"But look, as soon as I get all of my business straight, I'm gonna send you a check to help out with things."

"You don't have to do that, Ivan. We'll be fine."

"No, I want to do this. I *need* to. I... I owe you at least that much."

"Ivan, you don't owe me anything. You really don't."

"Yes, I do. It's my fault you ended up getting caught up with my father."

"No... I knew better. It's not your fault at all. And it's not all his fault, either. I made the decision to lay down with him, and I've paid for it. Believe me. You don't owe me anything. Take care of yourself. Okay, Ivan?"

"Toya—"

"Goodbye, Ivan. Talk to you soon, I hope."

Click.

I sat there and stared at the phone for a moment, feeling this strange sadness about leaving Latoya behind. I felt like I was repeating old sins or something. But that was crazy. We weren't dating or anything, and it wasn't like I loved her. My phone rang and startled me a little. I checked the screen to see that the call was coming from Earl.

"Hello?" I answered.

"Hey, man. What's going on? I'm leaving your mom's place right now. Your auntie said you were going back to Atlanta?"

"Yeah, man. It's time for me to head back."

"You couldn't call your boy and let him know? That's messed up, man."

"It was kinda last minute."

"Something came up?"

"You can say that…"

"Well, I hope everything's all right. What about the DUI? You got all that squared away?"

"Yeah. They were gonna suspend my license, but since I don't have an Arkansas license, they fined me instead. Paid my fine. Everything's cool."

"All right, well… stay in touch."

"I will, man. Hey, thanks for having my back."

"Anytime, man."

I hung up and suddenly had the urge to drink something, figuring that the effects would've worn off by the time I landed in Atlanta and had to drive home. I grabbed my newspaper and small carry-on bag and headed to the bar and grill that was just on the other side of the security checkpoint. I got a table, ordered a steak, and was nursing a drink when I saw her walk in with two other women. All three of them were wearing pant suits and sensible shoes. I figured they were her coworkers.

They sat about three tables over from mine, and I kept my eyes glued to her. When she glanced my way and finally noticed me, I nodded slightly, downed the rest of my drink, stood from my table, and headed over to hers. She looked up at me with a surprised expression on her face. My eyes narrowed as I said, "Donna. Haven't seen you in a while. Going on a trip?"

"A social work conference in Maryland," one of the other ladies informed me. She was a petite, light-skinned sister with short, natural hair. "Donna, who's your friend?" she added.

"Yeah, aren't you gonna introduce us?" the other lady asked. She was tall and thin with pale skin and blond hair.

I smiled at them. "I'm Ivan Spencer."

Both women dropped their eyes and said, "Oh," almost in unison.

Damn, I thought, *she told them, too?*

"Um, Ivan… this is Sherry," she said as she pointed to the sister. "And Liz."

"Nice to meet you ladies. Donna, can I speak to you for a moment?"

She hesitantly nodded and followed me over to the bar. "Yes?" she said with a little hostility in her voice.

"What the hell is wrong with you?" I said under my breath.

"What are you talking about?"

"You done told everybody in a hundred-mile radius that we slept together? Why would you do that?"

"Why would you play with me like that… like I was a toy or something? Do you know how I felt after I slept with you and you disappeared?" she said in a harsh whisper.

"You must've felt pretty good. After all, you did enjoy it, didn't you? You had to with all that moaning and screaming you did," I said with a smirk.

"You mean the sex? Yes, the sex was very good. You are excellent at that, Ivan. Excellent. The ignoring my calls and acting like I didn't exist afterwards? *That's* what sucked. *That* felt like crap."

"It was a one-night stand. Haven't you ever had one before? *Damn*."

"As a matter of fact, I haven't. And you never said it was going to be a one-night stand, Ivan. You know you didn't. If you had, you never would've gotten into my panties, that's for sure."

I stared at her for a moment.

"I liked you, Ivan. I mean I *really* liked you, and I thought you liked me. You acted like you did. You said all the right things. Made me feel special. Made me think you were a good guy. I fell for your act and gave you something that I don't give away easily—my body. You are the third man I've ever slept with in my entire life, Ivan. It was a mistake. A *big* one. And it hurt. It's my fault for falling for your act. You didn't force me to do anything. But you were still wrong to play with me like that. Dead wrong. Maybe I shouldn't have told everyone about us, but I was hurt. You have no idea how hurt I was. I hope no one ever hurts you like that."

"I... I apologized."

"Yeah, you did. And that was about as sincere as everything else you said to me."

She left and returned to her table before I could respond. I went back to my table, stared at my steak for a few minutes, paid my check, and left.

26

"Satisfaction"

After assessing the condition of my business and just how much money it had hemorrhaged while I was away, the first thought in my mind was that I needed a drink—a *strong* drink. Then I quickly chased that thought away as I realized I was dangerously close to becoming an alcoholic. But who the hell could blame me after everything I'd been through over the past weeks? As I stared at the bare facts in the form of numbers without the many zeros I was accustomed to, I realized I could use this situation to my advantage. If I was going to save my business, I'd have to put in the work. I was going to have to hustle the way I did when I first jumped into the real estate game. I was going to have to hit the pavement, make appearances at every high-rolling event I could gain entrance into. And the work, all of it, would occupy enough of my time and my mind to keep me from rehashing all that had happened in Arkansas. I'd make sure it did.

The only problem was I'd have to cut my assistant's hours, which meant some clients would have to reach my voicemail rather than a real person, but I had no choice. And besides, I was sure I could turn things around. If everything worked out the way I hoped, I'd be able to increase her hours. Hopefully, my client list would increase enough to require even more office staff.

My days were spent calling existing and former clients, assessing their needs, and seeking out referrals. I needed everybody who was anybody to know that Ivan Spencer was back and ready, willing, and able to take care of their real estate needs. And it worked. In under a month, my business was back on track and I was so busy, I didn't have time to think about my father or Erma or my mother. I didn't have time to think about the lies that had been told or the secrets that had been revealed. Thanks to an increased work load, I didn't have time to think about much of anything.

As a matter of fact, I didn't call home for more than a month. I didn't want to run the risk of Mama ending up on the phone and going into a demented rant in the middle of our conversation. But worse than that, I didn't want to run the risk of her happening to have a moment of clarity and sanity. How was I supposed to talk to her while she was in her right mind, knowing what I now knew? I wouldn't even know what to say to her. And I definitely wasn't going to waste my time, voice, or breath talking to my father and Erma.

The one person I thought of often and even thought about calling was Latoya. I wondered how she and her daughter were doing, if things were any better for her, any easier. I'd sent her a modest check, not much, but better than nothing. I never heard from her and was unsure if she'd received it. I wanted to call, but for some reason, I couldn't. I just couldn't.

Another side effect of all the work was that no one had shared my bed since I'd been back in Atlanta. It was either that I was too busy, too tired, or just plain bored with the overly made-up, expensively-dressed women I ran across. No one interested me or caught my eye. Alma even got wind of me being back in town and showed up unannounced at my door, and even with her pretty face and pretty body, she didn't move me. I was uninterested, to say the least. And it wasn't just because she was crazy. It was every woman I saw, every woman whose number was saved in my phone—none of them interested me. Not one.

That is, until I left my office late one night, realized I hadn't eaten dinner, stopped by a wing place to grab a bite to eat, and saw the girl behind the counter. She was short, shapely, and cute, and she reminded me of Latoya—from her smile to the way she wore her hair. She was younger than Latoya and me, but she was definitely grown. And I couldn't take my eyes off of her as she took my order. When she turned her back to me, my eyes damn near popped out of my head and I thought, *Yeah, she's definitely grown.*

I took a seat on the bench that sat next to the counter and waited for my order and tried not to stare at the woman whose name tag read, *Nikkesha.* I glanced at her a couple of times and noticed she was looking at me. When our eyes met, she smiled and something stirred inside of me. By the time my order was ready, I felt like I was going to explode. I handed her my credit card, signed the restaurant's copy of the receipt, turned over my copy, and slid it to her. "Why don't you put your phone number on the back of here so I can call you, *Nikkesha*?" I said, letting my eyes drag over her body from head to toe. Then I flashed her a lopsided grin.

She smiled, took the pen from my hand, scribbled something on the receipt, and handed it to me. "That's my phone number *and* my address. I get off in thirty minutes, and it takes me twenty minutes to get home."

I glanced down at the paper and slid it into my pocket. "Looks like I'll be seeing you in an hour, then." I turned to leave and added, "My name's Ivan, by the way."

She held up the restaurant's copy of my receipt. "I know, boo. I'll see you soon, I hope."

I raised an eyebrow and looked her over again. "Oh, you will."

***

Nikkesha lived in a neat little apartment in a complex in a decent neighborhood—not quite the hood but not far from it. It was decent enough that I wasn't too afraid of parking my car on the lot, but I wasn't comfortable with spending the night, either. I was going to enjoy a few hours with Nikkesha and head home long before the sun rose.

She greeted me at the door wearing a short, silky pajama set and a wide smile. "You actually came," she said, sounding both surprised and pleased. "I didn't think a brother like you would really mess around with a girl like me."

As I slid past her into her apartment, the scent of fragrant burning candles filled my nose. Soft music was streaming from the speakers of a small bookshelf stereo—soul music. "What do you mean 'a girl like you?'" I asked as she closed the door. I waited for her to move closer to me, slipped my arm around her waist, and kissed her. "You're just the kind of girl I like—a *fine* one."

"You fine, yourself, boo. *Real* fine."

I smiled down at her. "Thank you, baby."

She led me to the sofa and gently pushed me onto the soft cushion, then straddled my lap. Minutes later, we were well on our way to paradise when the song on the stereo changed, and Rita Holmes' voice filled my ears. With my lips locked with Nikkesha's, I froze. She lifted her head and stared at me with a slight frown. "What's wrong?"

I gripped her hips. "That song. Can you change the song?" I asked.

"Oh, that's it? You don't like the song?"

"No... I—can you just change it, please?" I was starting to get a little irritated.

"A'ight, boo. Hold on."

She climbed out of my lap and walked over to the stereo. A second later, Ron Isley was singing "Footsteps in the Dark." She reclaimed her seat in my lap and began plastering kisses on my face, neck, chest... and I just sat there. Hearing Rita Holmes' voice had extinguished the fire inside of me. The mood had lifted, and all I could wonder was if my father had been with Nikkesha, too. It was a crazy thought, but I couldn't get it out of my mind. I just couldn't.

I gently pushed against her shoulders and she looked up at me. "You don't like this song, either?"

I shook my head. "It's not that... I just—I can't do this."

She glanced down at my lap and cocked her head to the side. "Looks to me like you *can*, boo."

I shook my head again. "I'm sorry. I gotta go."

She jumped up from my lap in a huff and placed her hands on her waist. "You married, ain't you? Damn, the fine ones are always married."

I stood from her sofa and buttoned up my shirt. "No, I'm not married. It's complicated. I just need to go. I'm sorry."

Nikkesha glared at me as I left. No sooner than my feet hit the landing outside her door, I heard her utter a string of obscenities, and a second later, she slammed the door behind me.

I climbed into my car and sat there staring at Nikkesha's building for ten minutes before picking up my phone and dialing the number. When the groggy voice answered, I was tempted to hang up, but instead I said, "I didn't wake you up, did I?"

"Ivan, that you? What's going on? You okay?" Then I heard a soft voice in the background.

"Hey, man, tell your wife I'm sorry. I know it's late."

"It's okay. Hold on a sec, man," Earl said.

I closed my eyes and sunk into my seat. Less than a minute later, he returned to the phone. "What's up, man?"

"Hey, I'm sorry. I just... Things are messed up, man. Real messed up. My head's all jacked up. I got friends here, but we don't go back like me and you do, and I need someone to talk to."

"It's okay. What happened?"

I took a deep breath and told him about my father and all of the countless kids my mother said he'd fathered, including the one by Aunt Erma—me. I told him about the hatred I felt for him and Erma and the confusing feelings of anger, sadness, and love I felt for the woman who raised me as her own. I told him about my guilt for the way Latoya's life had turned out and finished with my encounter with Nikkesha and my confusion over it.

I could hear him lightly sigh into the phone. "That's a lot, Ivan. No wonder you called. Must've been hard to carry all of that around."

"Yeah, but I'm a man. I feel weak as hell right now. I should be able to handle this."

"Ivan, you're a human and what you just told me, all that stuff? It'd be hard for anyone to cope with—man or woman."

"Yeah, but the crazy thing is, I think I'm more upset about tonight. I mean, I... I never have trouble with that, you know? Shoot, I'm *known* for not having trouble with that."

"I'm a preacher, but you won't get struck down for saying the word 'sex' to me."

"Feels weird."

"Then forget I'm a preacher for a minute. You couldn't perform?"

"No, I mean, yes... I *could*. I mean, everything is working fine. I just couldn't get outta my head, you know? Started having these crazy thoughts about my daddy and all the women he's been with, started wondering if there was anyone I knew that he *hadn't* been with. Crazy, huh?"

"From what I know of your daddy's reputation, that's not crazy at all."

"Okay, but what am I supposed to do? Hell, if I can't have sex, what's left?"

"Maybe it's time for you to think about settling down and having a family."

"Excuse me, but hell, naw. I ain't built for that, bruh."

"I don't know why not. You hate your father for the way he treated your mother—"

"He still treats her like that."

"And you hate him for it. Why would you keep emulating him?"

I sat up straight and opened my eyes. "I ain't nothing like him! First of all, I don't even have a wife to disrespect. Second, I don't have a child in this world that I know of."

"But you use women."

"No, I don't!"

"Okay, tell me this: what were your plans with that girl tonight? Was this the start of a relationship, or were you gonna hit it and quit it?"

"That's an old term, Rev. It's played out."

"Answer the question, Ivan."

I shrugged. "Depends on how she was. We coulda hooked up on the long term if she was any good."

"Just long term sex? Nothing else?"

"Yeah."

"You don't think that's using her?"

"No. Hell, she invited me over. She wanted what I wanted. Was mad when I didn't give it to her. So if I was using her, she was using me, too."

"Two wrongs don't make a right, man. You know that."

I sighed. This was a mistake. I called to get that stuff off my chest, and it was turning into a damn afterschool special on promiscuity. "Look, I'ma let you go; thanks for listening. Sorry again for calling so late."

"I see you don't wanna hear what I have to say. But when you called me, knowing what I am, you shouldn't have expected me to tell you anything but what's right."

"I expected you to be my friend and understand."

"I *am* your friend, and I *do* understand. But sleeping with all these women, using them, that was cute when you were young and stupid. It was still wrong then, but now it's just ridiculous. If it's wrong for your father to do it, it's wrong for you to do it, too."

I closed my eyes again, didn't respond.

"You know I'm right. Deep down inside, you can see where your actions mirror your father's. Some people say we're doomed to repeat our parents' sins. But that's not true. You control your own actions and nobody else."

"I think I'm in love with Toya." I said it before I even realized it. Then I asked myself what was wrong with me.

"You *think* you are?"

"I think about her all the time, worry about her and her little girl. I wanna touch her so bad it's killing me, man. I think I love her, but I don't think I can be with her now."

"Why? I can tell you one thing: she feels the same way."

I frowned slightly, and at the same time felt a strange feeling deep inside of me. A warmth. "How would you know that?"

"I'm her pastor, Ivan. We talk often. Now I can't divulge the details of our conversations, but suffice it to say that she cares deeply about you. Always has."

"Even if that's true, if she really cares about me, I can't be with her. She... she was with my father, had a son by him. I don't think I can get past that. I'll always be thinking about it."

"If you love her, you'll move past it. You'll forgive, forget, and move on. Her son is grown."

"Forgive her? I forgave her a long time ago. I can't... I can't forgive myself."

"For what?"

"For leaving her behind and never looking back. I told you, I feel responsible for everything that happened to her. For her life."

"Ivan... Toya made those decisions. You can't blame yourself."

I sighed, felt my head tighten. "Yeah. Look, I need to go."

"Okay, man. Can I pray for you first?"

I held the phone, wanted to say no, but instead said, "O... okay."

"Heavenly Father," Earl began. "I come to You right now, first thanking You for my brother, Ivan. Lord, You know his heart. It's a good heart, Lord. I know You know that. He needs Your help. He needs for You to show him the way. He needs to see the true path clearly. Lord, guide him, show him the life You want him to lead. Make everything clear to him. In Jesus' name, amen."

"Amen," I said softly. Then I thanked him again, ended the call, and drove home.

27

"Each Day Gets Better"

Three months after my return to Atlanta, I finally called to check on things back home. When my father answered the phone, I almost dropped it. "Hello? Daddy?"

"Yeah, this Ivan?" he asked. Made me wonder how many other sons he had that called him at the house.

"Yeah, um… what're you doing there, answering the phone?"

"It's my house, ain't it? A man can't answer the phone in his own house?"

"Yeah, I guess…"

"I'm here with your mama, just like you wanted. I'm staying here again," he said, answering my unasked question.

"Oh, well… I know she's glad you're there."

"Hell, no she ain't. Been cussing me out since I walked in the door."

I smiled a little. "Oh, well, she does that sometimes."

"I know. Anyway, I'm here."

He kept repeating himself like he wanted me to jump up and down and cheer into the phone. Well, I wasn't going to congratulate him for doing exactly what a husband was supposed to do. "Where's

Erma?" I asked.

"She at her house. She'll be back after church Sunday so I can go fishing."

"Y'all got a little schedule going, huh?"

"Yeah, I guess you could say that."

"What about your woman, your little family over there in the trailer?" I asked.

"Humph, they all right."

Trouble in paradise? I wondered. I held the phone for a minute, and once I saw he wasn't going to elaborate, said, "How's Mama—other than cussing you out?"

"She about the same, done lost a little more weight, not eating too good, a little more confused. Been asking about you. Don't know if she want the grown you or the baby you, though."

"Can you put her on the phone?"

I heard him grunt, then the sound of shuffled footsteps echoed in the phone, and finally, Mama's voice sang, "Hello-o."

I smiled, felt a tug in my heart, and wondered how I ever could've been angry at her for what she did, for raising her sister's and her husband's love child as her own. She'd given me nothing but love my whole life. She was nothing but good to me. Yes, she'd lied, but the good she did, the care she'd given me, far outweighed that lie. "Hey, Mama. It's Ivan. How you feeling? You doing okay?"

"Ivan? This you? Boy, you sound good! How you doing, baby? When you coming home. Ain't seen you in years."

I rested my elbows on my desk as I held the phone to my ear. It was late, and I was in the office alone, thank goodness. I'd hate for anyone to see me in that condition—with tears in my eyes as I listened to my confused mother fire questions at me. "I'm good, Mama. I was just there a few months ago, remember?"

"No, can't say I do. It's so good to hear your voice, baby."

"It's good to hear yours, too, Mama."

"When you coming back? I'ma make you an apple stack cake when you get here. You know you love my apple stack cakes."

I smiled. "Yeah, I do, Mama. I'm coming home soon, I promise."

"Okay, baby. I love you from here to Heaven and back, Ivan."

I sighed at hearing her use a phrase she hadn't used since I was a boy. "I love you more than that, Mama."

***

The sound of my phone ringing startled me from a deep sleep to a fuzzy awareness. Checking the clock by my bed, I saw that it was 3:00 A.M. I'd only made it home from the office and fallen into bed an hour earlier. I rubbed my eyes, shook my head, and checked my phone's screen. It was an Arkansas number. An Arkansas number I hadn't saved and didn't know. My brain clicked, and all of the fuzziness faded away as one thought played in my mind: *something happened to Mama.*

"Hello?"

"Ivan? It's Toya."

"Toya… you must have a new number." I felt a little relieved, and then started to wonder if something had happened to Latoya or her daughter.

"Yeah, I do. Old one got cut off."

"Oh. Well, you okay? Everything all right?"

"Yeah... I'm sorry for calling so late. You were just... on my mind. You've been on my mind a lot lately."

"You've been on mine, too," I admitted.

"Really?"

I sat up on the side of the bed and nodded. "Yeah, I think about you all the time, Toya. You and your little girl. How is she?"

"A lot better. You know we're back home, now, and a nurse comes in every day. I'm really glad to have the help since Charles isn't here anymore."

I frowned slightly. "Where's Charles?"

"He left and went back up north. He said he hated it here. I didn't fight him on it. He's grown, and he needs to find his own way."

"Yeah. You get the check I sent?"

"Yes... thank you. You didn't have to do that."

"I *wanted* to."

There was a moment of silence, then she said, "Um... you said you think about me all the time, Ivan?"

"Yeah, I do, Toya. I really do."

"What do you think about?"

"Hmm, I think about your pretty face, your smile, your body."

"Is that it? Just the physical stuff?"

I closed my eyes. "No, baby. I think about a lot more than that."

"Like what?"

"Like your heart. I think about your heart, Toya."

"You think about me when you're with your girlfriends?"

With raised eyebrows, I said, "I don't have any girlfriends, Toya."

"Your booty calls?"

"None of those, either. I've actually been celibate since I got back here."

"You done found Jesus or something?"

I chuckled lightly. "Why you ask that?"

"Because that'd be the only way the famous Ivan Spencer could be celibate."

I lay back in my bed and gazed at the ceiling. "Famous? What am I famous for?"

"Breaking hearts."

There was a heavy silence between us for a few moments. "I'm sorry, Toya. I really am."

"I wasn't talking about me, Ivan. I meant everyone else."

I sighed. "Let me guess. You've been talking to Donna Whimper or her cousin or whoever, again."

"No, but you already know she's on the list."

I closed my eyes and after a couple of seconds said, "You know what, I'm sorry about Donna, and I'm sorry about anyone else I have ever hurt." My words surprised me, but what surprised me even more was that I meant them.

"That's good, Ivan. Hey, do you ever think about what it would be like for us to be together, like a couple?"

"All the time, Toya. But—"

"I understand. You can't get over my son being your brother."

I sighed lightly. "I'm sorry, Toya."

"Don't be. Well, I'll let you go. Goodnight, Ivan."

I held the phone for a second before saying, "Goodnight, Toya."

28

"Send it On"

A couple of weeks later, I was sitting in my office, not getting much of anything done. It was a Sunday and the office was closed, but I'd come in to catch up on some things. It was quiet, conducive for working, but I couldn't concentrate. My mind was wandering all over the place, and I had an extreme urge to call home, but I couldn't. No matter how many times I picked up my phone to dial the number, I always ended up laying it back on my desk. I didn't want to hear Erma tell me any more about how weak my mother had gotten or how much more confused she was or how time wasn't long for her anymore. I just didn't.

When the phone rang, I'd been staring at it for a full ten minutes. It startled me, and I wondered to myself if I had somehow willed it to ring as my parent's number appeared on the screen. Then the strangest thing happened. It stopped ringing. I mean, I let the call go to voicemail. Something in me wouldn't let me answer. When it began to ring again, my hand felt heavy as I lifted it to answer the call. It was all I could do to let the phone rest on the desk, hit the button, and activate the speakerphone. "Hello?" I said softly. There was a sound in my voice that was a little strange—fear, inexplicable fear.

"Ivan?" Erma's unsteady voice streamed from the phone's tiny speakers.

I closed my eyes and tried to close my ears, because I knew I didn't want to hear what she was about to tell me. I just knew it.

"Ivan?" she repeated, her voice even shakier.

"Yes?" I finally replied.

"Baby, I got some bad news. I... I don't know how to tell you this. I just don't know what to say."

"Just... just tell me," I said as I gripped my forehead. My heart was pounding at a rate akin to that of a jackhammer. My stomach bubbled as the remains of my lunch inched their way up my esophagus.

"Baby, it's your daddy. They found him this morning. He... he drowned."

I stared at the phone.

"Ivan?"

"What did you say?"

"Wardell—he'd been missing since he went fishing the other week. I didn't think nothing of it, because you know how he can disappear. I figured he ran back to that young girl or somebody else, you know? But we got the call from the sheriff's office a few minutes ago. I told them it didn't make no sense, because Wardell can swim. They said he might've had a heart attack or something and fell over in the lake. He's gone, Ivan. I'm so sorry, baby."

"He's... he's dead?"

"Yes, and Lord knows wasn't no love lost between me and him, but I never would've wished anything like this on him."

I wished I could say the same thing, but the truth was I couldn't. "Yeah." I closed my eyes again, rubbed my aching head. "Um, Aunt Erma, can you... do you think you could handle the arrangements for me? I know he had a burial plan. He and Mama had one together.

I don't... I don't think I can do it."

"Yes, I can do anything you need me to do. Ivan, you think I should tell your Mama?"

"I don't see what good it would do. She'll just forget, and you'll have to keep telling her over and over again."

"You're right. Well, let me go see if I can find that burial information somewhere around here. I'm sorry, again, Ivan."

"It's okay. Thanks, Aunt Erma."

I hung up and sat at my desk for several hours trying to put a finger on what I felt. Was it remorse or grief or sorrow? Was I still angry at him, or was I sad? I rested my head on my desk as the headache seemed to disappear all at once, and I fully realized what I was feeling—relief.

***

My father hadn't stepped foot in a church since the day he married my mother, since I was sure he and his *missus* didn't really take those kids to church that time. He didn't even attend me or Imogene's baptisms, believing that all church people were hypocrites and all preachers were crooks. At least that was what he always said. I personally thought he was afraid to attend church, afraid God would strike him down the second his sinful feet hit the floor of the sanctuary. If Earl hadn't been kind enough to offer his church for the services, my father would've had a graveside service, which would've been fine with me.

The day of his funeral was a rainy, gloomy day, but several people showed up, mostly women. As I sat on the pew, I glanced around at them and wondered how many of the sniffling, black-clad women had slept with the deceased. Then I told myself it would be easier to count the women he possibly *hadn't* slept with. Trying to tally up the number of his possible partners would take longer than the length of the service.

Aunt Erma sat next to me, and next to her sat Imogene and the elderly Pastor Bishop, who I had to admit looked pretty good for a septuagenarian. That wig he wore made him look at least sixty and if it weren't for the leisure suit he proudly wore, I might've given him fifty-nine. I'd met him at the house shortly before we all left for the funeral, and he seemed to be a nice man, and other than the fact that he sounded like he was preaching a sermon even during a regular conversation, I thought he might be someone I could grow to like.

I sighed as Imogene's whimpers filled the church. She was bent over holding a handkerchief to her trembling mouth as her husband slid a bony, wrinkled hand up and down her thick arm. "Oh, Daddy... *Daddy*," she moaned as if she didn't hate him as much as I did. He wasn't much of a father to either of us.

Aunt Erma wiped tears from her own eyes as she softly patted Imogene's thigh. "I know, sweetie, I know," she whispered.

And me? I just sat there with dry eyes and continued to wonder how many of my daddy's booty calls were in the room with us. I wondered how many of them had kids by him. I wondered how many of them had appeared on my mother's doorstep. I shifted my eyes to the open coffin and stared at the brown-skinned man in the black suit as he laid there appearing to be asleep, resting peacefully, and my blood began to boil. He didn't deserve to rest in peace after all he'd done. He'd been given the easy way out when my mother was left behind to suffer, a prisoner in her own mind.

I shifted on the pew and resisted the urge to leave. I didn't want to be there. I didn't want to pay my respects to this man. I didn't think I owed him any respect. No one did. Mama was at home with a caregiver since I didn't think it would make any sense to get her out of bed for a funeral she wouldn't even remember attending. I wished I'd stayed at the house with her.

When his baby mama, the one he left my mother for, entered the sanctuary with her tribe, I just shook my head. She was dressed in all black, including a hat and a veil, giving the appearance of a grieving widow. She eased into a pew on the side opposite the one reserved for family, and I was grateful she had at least that much sense. I glanced at Aunt Erma and noticed her eyes narrowing as she spotted the woman and her children. Shortly after they arrived, Latoya walked into the sanctuary. Our eyes locked as she took a seat across the aisle from me. I wished I could sit with her and hold her hand. I'd missed her.

When Rita Holmes sashayed down the aisle wearing a modest black dress and sat down next to Latoya, I turned my head. My father's life was the same in death as it had been in life, surrounded by skanks. I slumped down in the pew and hoped the service would speed by, but I knew better.

After the choir sang a mournful version of "Amazing Grace" and Earl offered the world's longest prayer, two ancient deacons stood at the front of the church and offered words of encouragement before sharing one scripture each from the New and Old Testaments. Then came more choir music. When folks started coming to the front of the church, talking about what a good man my father was, I wanted to laugh. Instead, I just sat there and stared into space and let my eyes glaze over. By the time the service was over, I was damn near asleep. Erma had to shake me a little just so I would stand and leave with the rest of the family.

I watched them lower my father into the ground and followed my family back over to the church for repast. By then, the crowd of funeral-goers had thinned out a lot, leaving mostly family behind. I was glad to see Latoya there, even gladder when she sat next to me. We chatted a little—she offered me her condolences, and I just thanked her for being there. That was truly the highlight of my day. Just being there with her, seeing her lovely face, hearing her talk about her daughter's progress, all of that made things better.

When she stood to throw our paper plates away, I watched her, the way she walked, the way her braids fell to the middle of her back. I thought about her smile, the warmth in her eyes, and I realized why I couldn't get her out of my mind when we were apart. Latoya was *real*. She was a genuinely good person, and her heart was pure. She'd never asked me for anything, nothing at all. And of all the people in the world, I owed her. I truly did. I should've come back for her, married her, given her the good life. She was my first and only love. And without her even saying it, I knew she still loved me. I knew she always had.

I'd spent most of my life comparing women to the fabled Mrs. Roundtree, believing she was the perfect woman. But truthfully, no one had compared to Latoya, and deep inside, I knew no one ever would.

She made it back to the table and smiled at me. "Did you miss me?" she asked with a flutter of her eyelashes.

I returned her smile. "I always do, Toya. Thanks again for coming. I know it couldn't have been easy with what happened in the past."

She dropped her eyes. "It's okay. I wanted to be here for you."

I reached for her hand and gently squeezed it in mine. "Well, you made my day."

She looked up at me. "I'm glad I did."

"I just wanted to make sure I gave you my condolences, sugar," a voice said, intruding on our private moment.

I looked up and wanted to scream. Rita Holmes was standing over us with a sincere expression on her face. It appeared that she'd adjusted the neckline of her modest dress to show all of her cleavage.

"Thank you," I grunted softly.

"You know you're welcome, sugar."

"Aren't you the one who sang a solo?" Latoya asked. "You have an amazing voice!"

Rita fanned herself. "Thank you. That song has been on my heart ever since I heard about Wardell's passing. I'm so glad the pastor let me sing it."

"Me, too! Didn't her song touch you, Ivan?" Latoya gushed.

"Mm-hmm," I said.

Rita rested her hand on my arm, squeezed it gently, and leaned in close. "I sure hope you'll drop by my place again soon."

And with that, she flounced out of the church's small cafeteria.

"What place is she talking about?" Latoya asked.

"She's got a restaurant I stumbled upon one day."

"Oh…" She turned and looked around the room.

I leaned in close to Latoya. "I slept with her. I'm sorry."

Latoya's head snapped around, and her eyes locked with mine. "Well, I figured *that*."

"You figured it? How?"

She lifted both eyebrows and gave me a smirk. "Well, it might've been the way she was groping your arm or the way she shoved her breasts in your face."

"Oh…"

"Mm-hmm. Anyway, why'd you apologize to me for it?"

I shrugged. "I feel bad about it."

"Well, you don't need to apologize to me. But you might wanna repent or something."

I nodded, unsure of what to say next.

"Well, I'ma get back home to my girl and relieve my cousin," she said, standing from her seat. She smiled down at me. "Talk to you later, Ivan. Take care."

"Your cousin? It's good you've got someone helping you."

"Yeah… well, bye, Ivan."

"Bye, Toya." I watched her walk out and wondered to myself why I felt so bad about her saying "take care" and "bye" to me.

I was sitting there with a frown, staring at the door she'd disappeared through, when I felt a tap on my shoulder.

"Uh-ruh, brother-in-law, would you mind passing me that blessed salt shaker?"

I turned to face Pastor Bishop as he sermonized his request. I nodded and handed him the salt.

"Praise God, brother-in-law. Ha! Woo, Lord! This is some good food right 'chea!"

I nodded again and stood to leave before he could lean back in his seat, wipe his mouth with a handkerchief, and begin to praise God for the doggone silverware.

***

I sat in my mother's room after the funeral, watching her sleep, taking in her frail appearance, and wondering how long it would be before I'd have to watch her be lowered into the ground. I stared at her for a long time, fell asleep at her bedside. It was Erma who gently woke me up and suggested I go to bed and get some real sleep since my flight left early the next morning. I nodded and shuffled to my room. She followed me and stood at my door as I stripped down to my t-shirt and boxers.

I sat on my bed and said, "You need something?"

She stepped into the room. "Um… Imogene and her husband left."

I nodded. "Okay. Hope they have a safe trip."

She stood there for a moment with her eyes downcast. "You still mad at me?" she finally asked softly.

I sighed as I ran my hands over my head. "I don't know how I feel. Maybe not angry anymore, just… just disappointed."

"I can understand that." She turned to leave.

"Hey, can I ask you something?"

She nodded and faced me. "Anything."

"How'd y'all keep it a secret for so long? I mean, I can't believe no one ever told me. Folks had to know you were pregnant. They had to know Mama wasn't."

She leaned against the door facing and folded her arms over her chest. "We come from a different time—me, Versie, and Wardell. Folks our age kept to themselves, minded they own business. Wasn't nobody running around telling they own business, either. That was unheard of back then. I stayed inside for the most part when I was pregnant. So did Versie. I even stopped working, and Versie stopped going to church. I'm sure folks knew, but they also knew not to ask. There was rumors, but we didn't confirm a thing. If we said you was Versie's baby, that's what they accepted. I'da swore to it in court if I'd had to and dared somebody to say I was lying. But no one ever questioned us, because Versie never treated you like nothing but her own."

"Does Imogene know?"

"Not unless you told her. Me and Versie and Wardell was supposed to take this to the grave."

"Who named me?"

"Versie did. From the moment I had you, you were hers, Ivan. I really hope you can get that. You are her child, and she was a good mother. The best. I'll never take that away from her."

"But you loved me?"

She walked over to me and placed her small hand on my cheek. "I still do, baby boy. With all my heart. And I always will. I am so proud of you, of the man you are, of how you take care of Versie. Giving you away was the hardest thing I've ever had to do, but seeing how you turned out, I know it was the best thing." She leaned in and kissed my forehead. Then she left my room.

29

"Show Me"

In the two weeks since my father was laid to rest, I hadn't slept a wink. Not a single, solitary second. And it was driving me crazy. I was too exhausted to think, couldn't really get any work done. And I'd started drinking again. My mind was racing so much, I was willing to do anything to settle it down. But even drunk, I still couldn't sleep. I was afraid I was losing my mind.

I was so desperate, I called Earl and asked him to pray for me. I called him one Saturday afternoon, hoping he'd say a quick prayer and let me go. But no such luck.

"Hey, thanks for the prayer, man. I appreciate it," I said.

"Anytime. Look, can I say something?"

I glanced around my empty office. "Um… Earl, I'm really busy right now… got an appointment coming in soon, too." That much was true. I really did have an appointment coming up.

"Only take a minute or two."

I groaned lightly.

"I know you don't wanna hear it, but you need to hear it. I'm glad I was able to pray for you, but I'd be less than a man of God if I didn't share what's on my heart."

I sighed. "Go ahead, man."

"You need to forgive your father so you can let go of this guilt that's eating at you."

I leaned back in my chair. "I don't feel no guilt about my father."

"Yes, you do. That's why you can't sleep."

"Man, you must be crazy."

"Ivan, I've been a pastor for a while now. I've talked to a lot of troubled people, people who couldn't sleep. And every last one of those people was harboring guilt about something. Guilt will eat away at you, destroy you if you let it."

"So you think I'm feeling guilty about not forgiving my father before he died."

"Yes, I *know* you are. You loved him."

"Humph."

"You did, Ivan. You've spent your life trying to be like him, whether you realize it or not. I think you idolized him in a way. And your heart can't deal with the way things ended between you and him."

Marjorie, my assistant, peeked her head in the door and whispered, "Your one o'clock is here, Mr. Spencer."

I nodded and held up a finger. "Look, I really gotta go. Thanks, again." I hung up before giving him a chance to respond.

I walked into the reception area and retrieved who I hoped would be my newest client. After we shook hands and took our seats in my office, I gave her a smile and said, "How can I help you, Mrs. Joshua?"

"Actually, it's *Reverend* Joshua. See, I'm starting my own church here in Atlanta, and I need to find a building in a nice part of town where the neighbors won't mind if things get a little loud. My church will be Pentecostal, you see."

I nodded and pulled out a folder my assistant had already prepared for the meeting. "Yes, Reverend. I have some properties here for you to peruse. I'm certain you'll be able to find what you need here."

I walked around my desk and as I began to lay the pictures before her, she grasped my wrist. I frowned slightly as I looked down at her. She was tiny and seemed to have once been a pretty lady. But her beauty was hidden behind thick glasses and a stern expression at that moment. "Is something wrong?" I asked.

She shook her head and moaned softly. "Nothing is wrong with *me*, but the sorrow is thick in this place. I can feel it down in my *soul*." She released my wrist and stood from the chair. As she paced my office, I backed away from her and rubbed my wrist. That little old lady had a grip on her.

"Mmm, Father God, help him!" she shouted.

My frown deepened as I fell into my chair and stared at her, wondering if I should call for help.

Then she stopped dead in her tracks and stared at me. "He loved you. He wasn't perfect, but he loved you. And you loved him. You really did."

"Ma'am?"

She smiled. "Good manners. She raised you well."

I just stared at her, confused and intrigued at the same time.

"Let it go, child. All of the anger, the hurt feelings. Let it go. They loved you, and they did the best they could. They weren't perfect, they did a lot of wrong, but they loved you and that was the one thing that made the difference. They loved you—*all* of them loved you." She walked over to me and rested her hand on my arm. "Forgive them, forgive yourself, and make things right."

With a wrinkled brow, I said, "Make things right?"

"Just think about it, and pray about it, child. Talk to God. You know Him, you learned of Him when you were a child, didn't you?"

I nodded. "Yes, ma'am," I said, thinking of my baptism and all of the years Mama dragged me to church.

"Pray, child, and then you'll know what you need to do, and you need to do it *now*." She picked up the photos and stacked them in front of me on my desk. "I'll call and reschedule."

And with that, she left.

***

That night as I lay in my bed, my mind was still troubled. I didn't know what to make of what had happened in my office with Reverend Joshua. And I still felt skeptical about what Earl had said about me feeling guilty for not forgiving Daddy. If that was true, I'd never sleep again. How could I forgive a dead person?

"In your heart."

I sat up in bed and glanced around the room. I'd heard the words, but were they just in my head, or had someone else said them? I shook my head, figuring that the lack of sleep was making me crazy. I lay back on my pillow and closed my eyes.

"Forgive him in your heart."

There was that voice again. This time, I stood from the bed. I just stood there, trying to figure out what was going on. "God, is that you?" I asked aloud. Then I shook my head again. *Why did I say that?* I picked up the phone to call Earl to ask for more prayer, and heard, *"You can pray for yourself."*

I dropped the phone, fell to my knees, and did something I hadn't done since I was a little boy sitting at the dinner table or at bedtime with my mother. I prayed. I asked God to show me what to do, how to make things right, as Rev. Joshua had said. I closed my eyes and talked to God like He was in the room with me, like He was someone I knew, because that was what felt right. Besides, He *was* in the room with me... kind of.

I told Him about my problems, asked Him to forgive my sins and to help me, and for the first time in a long time, everything in my life became clear to me. I knew exactly what I needed to do, what steps to take, and I was thankful that when I climbed back into bed and closed my eyes, I had no trouble falling asleep.

30

"Save Room"

I walked into the house to the sound of laughter. I recognized the voices—my mother's and Aunt Erma's. I smiled as I made my way through the small house, dragging my suitcase behind me.

"What y'all laughing at?" I said as I entered the kitchen where they were seated at the table.

"Ivan?!" Erma exclaimed. I think she wanted to hug me but was afraid to. So I walked over to her and wrapped my arm around her shoulder.

"Good to see you, Auntie," I said.

She smiled up at me, but I could see tears forming in her eyes. "I didn't know you were coming. We haven't heard from you in weeks."

I leaned over and kissed my mother on the forehead. "I know. I'm sorry about that. I had some stuff to take care of, but I'm here now. Here to stay."

A look of shock spread across Erma's face as she looked over at Mama. "You hear that, Versie? Ivan say he's here for good."

"Ivan?" Mama said, as if just realizing I was in the room, as if she'd been absent when I kissed her. "Hey, baby! We was just talking about you, about how you used to chase them little girls around the church. I knew then you was gon' be like Wardell."

I stiffened a little. My trip to my daddy's grave and the forgiving words I'd offered to him hadn't totally taken the strain of our relationship away. But I had finally admitted to myself that I had lived my life much like my father had. He'd influenced me in a lot of ways, from my swagger to my confidence to the way I treated women in the past. And he'd blessed me with his looks. But the good thing was that my sweet mother had influenced me even more, she'd shown me how to love unconditionally and selflessly. I gave Mama a slight smile and said, "Yes, ma'am."

"I wonder where he is. Sure could eat some ribs right about now," she said as she rubbed her stomach.

I stood from the table. "How about I put my bag in my room and then go and get you some ribs? That sound good, Mama?"

She grinned. "Yes, baby!"

I kissed her cheek and left the kitchen. Erma followed me to my room. "You say you're here to stay?" she asked.

I nodded as I turned to face her. "Yes, ma'am. You can go home today if you want. Is the aide here?"

"Yeah, she's cleaning up Versie's room. Um, what about your business and everything?"

I laid my suitcase on my bed. "I sold it."

"What? Why?"

"Because I need to be here with my mother right now. I need to spend as much time with her as I can."

She nodded.

I stared at her for a moment. "I forgive you, and I want to thank you for giving me to her. I couldn't have asked for a better mother.

You did the right thing."

She looked up at me as a tear trickled down her face. I wrapped my arms around her and hugged her tiny frame tightly. "Thank you, Aunt Erma," I whispered.

I released her as she wiped her eyes with the back of her hand.

"I'm gonna go get Mama those ribs, but I'll be gone for a while. Got some errands to run."

"I'll be here. I'm not going nowhere. I like being here with Versie."

I smiled and gave her a nod.

A few minutes later, I was headed down the dirt road in the Honda I had bought and driven to Arkansas after I sold my Mercedes. I pulled into the driveway, stepped onto the porch, and watched the screen door wiggle as I knocked on it. The front door opened and surprise registered on her face.

"Hey, look, I just wanted to give you this. I hope it helps at least a little," I said.

Ebony, my father's baby mama, took the check from me, looked at it, and with wide eyes said, "Thank you."

"And, I... uh, wanna apologize for coming around here so much, beating on your door and stuff."

She stared down at the check. "It's... okay."

"Hey, um... you think I could come back and get my daddy's grill?"

She nodded. "Yeah, that'll be fine."

"All right. Thanks," I said. Then I left.

In the car, on the way to my next destination, I pulled out my cell phone and dialed a number I hadn't dialed in a long time. I hoped it hadn't changed.

I was relieved when I heard, "Hello?"

"Hey, Donna, this is Ivan Spencer. Before you hang up, I just have one thing I need to say."

After a long pause, she said, "Okay."

"I'm sorry for treating you the way I did, and I mean that from the bottom of my heart. I was wrong, and I hope you find a man worthy of you one day, because you are truly something special."

"Okay… um, thank you."

"No, thank *you*."

"For… for what?"

"For helping me to become a better man. You take care, okay?"

"Okay… uh… you, too, Ivan."

By the time our call had ended, I was pulling into her driveway. My heart was beating furiously in my chest, and my hand shook when I opened the car door. I took a deep breath as I made my way to the house. I knocked and waited and silently prayed that my words would be received well.

An angel opened the door and smiled at me. "Ivan?!"

I returned her smile, squeezed through the half-open door, and pulled her into my arms. I kissed her deeply, and when we separated, I held her face in my hands, and said, "Toya… Toya, Toya, Toya. *Oh, Toya…*"

She gave me a look that was somewhere between delight and

surprise. "Ivan… what—"

"Toya… baby, I love you. Maybe I always have. I'm not sure about that, but I'm sure about how I feel right now. And I know I love you, baby. I ain't perfect, I got some issues, but I truly love you. I don't wanna waste any more time, okay?"

She gave me a bewildered look. "But you—"

"I sold my business and my condo and my car. I'm here to stay, and I need to be with you. You understand that?"

She nodded. "But—"

"And I wanna be here for you and your little girl. I wanna take care of y'all. With what I received from selling my business and the royalties I still get from my music, I have enough money to make sure she's taken care of the right way, with nurses and stuff. And I can rebuild my business here, too. I want you to get some rest. I'm gonna take care of you, of both of you, and I don't ever want you to have to worry about money again. I love you, Toya, and I wanna be with you and nobody else. Do you love me? Tell me you love me."

As tears trickled down her cheeks, she said, "Yes, I do. I do love you, Ivan. I've… I've always loved you. But this is all so much. Are you sure? I mean, I thought you—"

"I've never been more sure of anything in my life, baby. And if you're worried about what happened between you and my father, I don't care about that, anymore. I love you too much to be concerned about that."

She smiled as I wiped her tears with my hand. "Then what do we do? Where do we start?" she asked.

"You can start by properly introducing me to your little girl. And we can go from there. I just want to be in your life for the rest of your life, for the rest of my life. I just want to love you, okay? I want you to be my wife. I want us to have more kids and stuff. Is that okay with you?"

She giggled lightly and then she reached up and kissed me. "Yes, all of that is okay with me."

I rested my forehead against hers and said, "I love you so much, Toya."

She wiped a single tear from my cheek and said, "I love you, too."

For information regarding Alzheimer's disease and caregiver support groups, visit:

http://www.alz.org/apps/we_can_help/support_groups.asp

Learn about resources for parents of children with disabilities here:

http://www.supportforfamilies.org/internetguide/index.html

For more information about Adrienne Thompson, visit:

http://adriennethompsonwrites.webs.com

Sign up for Adrienne's newsletter here: http://eepurl.com/jnDmH

Follow Adrienne on Twitter!

https://twitter.com/A_H_Thompson

Like Adrienne on Facebook!

https://www.facebook.com/AdrienneThompsonWrites

Follow Adrienne on Pinterest!

http://www.pinterest.com/ahthompsn/

Also by Adrienne Thompson:

Fiction Series:

The *Bluesday* Series:

Bluesday

Lovely Blues

Blues In The Key Of B

Locked out of Heaven (Tomeka's Story – A Bluesday Continuation)

The *Been So Long* Series:

Rapture (A Been So Long Prequel)

If (Wasif's Story) A Been So Long Prequel

Been So Long

Little Sister (Cleo's Story—a companion novel to Been So Long)

Been So Long 2 (Body and Soul)

Been So Long III (Whatever It Takes)

The *Your Love Is King* Series

Your Love Is King

Better

Stand-alone novels:

Ain't Nobody

See Me

When You've Been Blessed (Feels Like Heaven)

Nonfiction Titles:

Just Between Us (Inspiring Stories by Women) –as a contributor

Seven Days of Change (A Flash Devotional)

All books are available at amazon.com, barnesandnoble.com, **and** kobobooks.com

Please enjoy this excerpt from *Bluesday*
(Now available in Kindle, Nook, Kobo, and paperback)

I smiled as the crowd roared in response. "Alright, this next song is dedicated to my man. Any of y'all wanna be my man tonight?" The crowd roared again. I walked over to Will, who'd left his post behind the drums. Like I did at that point in every show, I chose a member of the audience to serenade. A little trick I'd picked up from Ms. Janet Jackson. Will nodded and went down into the crowd.

I'd chosen a tall, dark brown-skinned brother who wore his hair in neat cornrows. He was wearing jeans and an over-sized polo. His eyes were stretched wide as Willie escorted him onstage. "Hey, be cool," Willie said into his ear. "And hands off." Willie gave him a look that said, *I'm not playing.* The guy nodded and took a seat in the chair provided for him.

I leaned in close to him and smiled seductively. "Hey, baby. What's your name?" I said into the microphone.

"Bruce," he said, eyeing me like a piece of candy.

"Well Bruce, this one's for you." I slowly and softly kissed him. I didn't usually do that, but what the hell? He looked harmless enough. The crowd roared again. Jealous men shouted comments. Bruce's eyes widened and I saw them dart towards Willie as if to say, *I didn't do it, she did.*

I gave the signal, and as Zeke began a soulful guitar intro into "So

Bad," I kneeled in front of Bruce and placed my hands on his knees. I waited for the drums and keyboard to join him, and then I closed my eyes and began to sing:

"I gotta man, he sho' does treat me bad
Spend all my time, alone, lonely, and sad
Wake up at night, he's gone, don't know where
And when I cry he don't even seem to care

But I tell you this, I can't leave him alone
Cause his kinda lovin' is the only lovin' I know

Can't somebody tell me, why he treats me so bad
I just wanna know, what I did to make him mad
Please tell me, why he treats me so bad
If you tell me, I'll try to fix it real fast..."

The lyrics touched my soul like they never had before and I felt something rising up inside of me. As I continued to sing, I felt the tears as they rolled down my face. I had cried plenty of times before, but this time I felt an ache I can't explain. It was almost as painful as the day my daddy died, because at that moment, I felt like my marriage had died, too. I shook my head and sang the words which echoed my real-life situation. I sang and sang until it felt like everything inside of me was emptied out, and then the song ended. I wiped my face as the audience exploded in loud applause, believing that they had just witnessed a heart rending performance, not realizing that the pain I'd portrayed and tears I had shed were all too real.

I opened my eyes and Bruce was staring at me, tears in his own eyes. I'd touched him. I stood up and took his hand. I hugged him. He kept his arms beside him at first, heeding Willie's warning. Then he returned my embrace. Willie stepped forward to escort him back into the crowd.

I covered the microphone with my hand. "You here with a date?" I asked.

Bruce's eyes widened again and he shook his head. At that point, it probably wouldn't have mattered to him if he *was* with a date.

I turned to Willie. "Take him backstage." I've never done that before either.

Willie frowned. "What?"

"Take him backstage. I wanna talk to him after the show."

Willie shrugged. "It's your world. Come on, man." I watched them disappear backstage and then Willie reappeared behind the drums.

"Alright, now that I got me a man, let's party, y'all!" I screamed.

The crowd seemed more than willing to party with me. I continued my show, one of my best, I must say, and then headed backstage to my dressing room.

Bruce was standing just beyond the curtains, where he'd watched the remainder of the show. I grabbed his hand and led him to my dressing room. I closed the door behind us and pushed him onto the small loveseat. He looked at me like it was the first time he'd seen a woman, like he'd discovered some new, wonderful treasure.

"How old are you, Bruce?" I asked as I straddled his lap.

"Uh... uh, twenty?" he said as if he wasn't at all sure.

"Really? Young for a blues fan, ain't you?" I said as my lips hovered over his.

"Uh, my... my mama likes blues." I guess he meant that she'd turned him onto the blues, like my daddy had me.

I inspected his face. In the dim light of the dressing room, he looked even younger than twenty. Smooth brown skin and the shadow of a mustache gave him away. Eighteen maybe? Whatever. It didn't matter.

I kissed Bruce, hard this time. He sat there, stiff as a board at first, and then instinct kicked in. He placed his hands on my hips and began to kiss me back. He wasn't a half-bad kisser either. I wrapped my arms around him and waited for my better judgment to kick in. I waited for the voice in my head to tell me to stop, that I was a married woman, and that this was wrong. I never heard it. I ended the kiss and looked at Bruce. He was breathing hard. I don't know if it was the liquor, or the fact that I just needed someone, but I kissed him again. This time, he placed his hands on my back and eased them down to my behind. I didn't stop him. I undressed him, still listening closely for that voice of reason to shout at me. Silence. I gave Bruce what every other male fan wanted. I gave him a night he'd never forget, a story he'd tell over and over again like an old soldier telling war stories.

I took my sweet time and seduced him in my dressing room, and then I took him up to my suite and seduced him two more times.

Maybe I wanted Clyde to catch me. I don't know. All I know is that when Bruce left my suite the next morning, he was wearing a big smile and the scent of my Beyoncé Heat cologne all over his body. With an autographed CD in hand, he thanked me and headed out the door. In my hand, I held a slip of paper with his phone number. I looked across the room at the trash can which held empty foil wrappers, the only evidence of the night before. I sat on the side of the bed and cried.